Nep
Secret Code

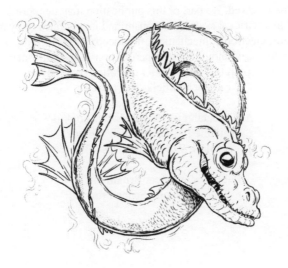

by Genna Rowbotham

Illustrated by Terry Cooper

Neptune's Secret Code

All text copyright © Genna Rowbotham 2024
Illustrations by Terry Cooper

A CIP catalogue record for this book is
available from the British Library.
ISBN: 978-1-7398474-8-7

Published in Great Britain in 2024
by Adventure Scape Press

For my wonderful husband, Craig.
And Charlie, Holly, and Beatrice
who continue to inspire me.

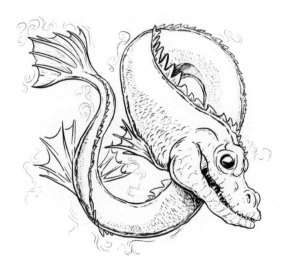

Chapter One

Hannah and her mum stepped off the train at Morvoren Station. Nervously, she brushed some fluff off her leggings and pulled at the hem of her t-shirt, twisting it around her finger. So. This was it. Cornwall. For the entire summer. Her best friend, Becky, would have leapt at the chance – but not her. She'd rather be tidying her messy bedroom – and she hated doing that!

Behind them, Dad was making funny noises as he wrestled her floral suitcase onto the platform. 'Blimey, Hannah! What've you got in here?'

'Just clothes and…' She paused. 'Stuff.'

'Stuff!' Dad chuckled.

Hannah looked up at him. Why did he laugh at things that weren't even funny? 'It's Becky; she helped me pack. Six weeks is a long time to be away from home, you know.'

'I'm sorry, love. I wish you could come with us, but it's a business trip.' Mum sniffled, covering her nose with her hand. 'Besides, you'll have an amazing time staying with Auntie Meg. I think she gets quite lonely in the cottage.'

'Yeah, yeah… I'm sure I'll be fine,' mumbled Hannah. Although she wasn't fine. She wasn't fine at all.

Just then, Auntie Meg zipped through the crowd towards them, wearing leopard print sunglasses that nearly covered her entire face. 'Hello!' she boomed, loud enough to stir some passers-by.

'Hi, Meg!' said Mum, embracing her with a

hug and a kiss. 'Thanks so much for looking after our Hannah.'

Auntie Meg took off her sunglasses. 'Oh, it's my pleasure!' she said, her eyes twinkling at Hannah. 'We're going to have a fun time, aren't we, love?'

Hannah wasn't so sure, but she returned her a smile anyway.

'Have you got time for a drink?' Auntie Meg asked Mum.

'Yes, sure!' said Mum, heading towards the station café.

Hannah hadn't seen her auntie for a long time because she lived so far away, but Mum had always said she couldn't have wished for a nicer big sister.

The café was busy and noisy chatter filled the air. When they finally found a spare table, Mum and Auntie Meg were talking non-stop as if they hadn't spoken to each other in years – although it was only last night that they'd been chatting on the phone for almost an hour.

Dad tried cheering Hannah up by telling her some not-so-funny jokes, but she wasn't in the mood – so she played another game on her mum's borrowed phone.

After glancing at his watch, Dad plonked his empty cup on the table and then gave a loud cough to interrupt Mum's chatter. 'We'll miss our train, love if we don't go.'

'Yes, I know, I'm coming.' Mum stood and stretched her arms towards Hannah. 'Come here – give us a cuddle.'

But Hannah didn't feel like cuddling. Still, she loosely wrapped her arms around Mum and said, 'Enjoy your business trip.'

'Thanks, love.' Mum cupped Hannah's face with her hands to kiss her. 'Oh… I'm going to miss you.'

'Really?' Hannah's voice wobbled.

'Of course, I will!' said Mum, sounding offended. 'But the weeks will soon fly by, and I'll call you every day to hear about all the fun you've had.'

Hannah stared up at Mum, wishing she'd change her mind – but it didn't look likely. She was already rummaging in her bag for their train tickets.

Dad cleared his throat. 'Look after yourself.'

'Yeah, sure… Seeya then.' Hannah gave him a half-hearted hug and then took one step back, preparing herself for the pain of being left behind.

There was an awkward silence before Mum and Dad headed to their platform, occasionally turning around to wave until they disappeared through the crowd.

'Come on, love,' said Auntie Meg, pushing Hannah's suitcase on a trolly through the busy crowd towards the car park. 'Let's go and have our own adventure!'

Lots of people were hurrying in different directions. Girls about the same age as Hannah buzzed past – seemingly excited. Maybe some were going on their holidays… But it didn't feel like a holiday to her. Nevertheless, she managed to put on a brave face and made an effort for her auntie. After all, she did seem thrilled to be spending some time together.

Auntie Meg pressed a button on her car keys and the roof folded down on her bright-blue sports car.

'Ooh, very nice!' exclaimed Hannah, stroking the door. 'And shiny!'

'Thank you,' said her auntie, smiling as they climbed into the front seats. 'You might like to know I've got a new pet for company.'

'Really!'

Auntie Meg laughed. 'Really!'

Hannah had always wanted a pet of her own, but Mum always said, "When you're old enough to look after it." Even though she was ten years old now and totally capable.

'What kind of pet is it?'

'He's a little kitten,' said Auntie Meg with a smile.

'Ah, cool! Can't wait to meet him.'

'That's good!' said Auntie Meg, chuckling. 'You can help each other settle in.'

The gentle wind blew through Hannah's hair as she watched the cars whizz by on the opposite side of the dual carriageway. Auntie Meg sped along too until the traffic built up, forcing her to slow down. But it didn't matter. Although Hannah was looking forward to seeing the new kitten, she was in no rush to arrive.

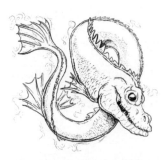

Chapter Two

So, this must be Morvoren. Yes, Hannah had a
vague memory of it from last time, but it was five
years ago now. There were lots of shops and
restaurants… and people with beach bags
wandering around. Some of them had probably been
there…. The beach. She shuddered just thinking
about it. Well, she definitely wouldn't be going.

Her auntie drove over a steep hill that led to a
narrow road – and then… There it was – the sea!
Sparkling in the distance through the trees.
Hannah's stomach spun like a hamster on a wheel,
so she tore her gaze away as Auntie Meg drove

round a sharp bend. Phew! Thank goodness she couldn't see it anymore.

'And – we're here!' announced Auntie Meg as she drove onto the driveway, gravel crunching under the tyres.

Hannah sat for a moment… She felt excited to meet the little kitty yet scared at the same time. The journey had reminded her of how close to the sea they actually were – and she was in no rush to get out of the car. At least her auntie wasn't nagging her to get a move on, but she couldn't stay there forever.

Forcing herself to climb out, she stared up at the picturesque white cottage. It was way too close to the edge of the cliff for her liking. And over the edge of the cliff… The sand and the sea. *Ugh*… she began to feel sick. Quickly, she looked away, staring at the pretty flowers in the garden instead. But she could hear the waves smashing against the cliffs down below, so she covered her ears and began to hum.

By this time, Auntie Meg had already opened the front door and abandoned Hannah's suitcase in the hallway with a thud. 'Are you alright?' She stared at her from the doorway as though Hannah had gone mad. 'What's the matter?'

'Nothing,' said Hannah, pulling her hands away from her ears.

'Well, come on in then, someone's waiting to see you.'

'OK, I'm coming.' Hannah strolled up the garden path, her stomach still swirling. Truth was, it did look like the perfect beach holiday home – but not for her. Not here. Where that horrible accident had happened…

What if the tide came in and the beach got flooded? she worried. *What if the cliffs crumbled and the cottage fell into the sea? What if…*

Just then a tiny white kitten pitter-pattered towards Hannah and looked up at her with a cute 'Meow!' before playfully circling her legs.

'Aww! Hello, little kitty!' As she picked him up and drew him close, his big blue eyes sparkled back at her. 'Oh, he's so cute!'

'He is, isn't he?' Auntie Meg grinned. 'I haven't thought of a name for him yet though.'

'Ooh – can I name him?' Hannah squealed with delight.

'Course you can!'

Holding the kitten at arm's length, Hannah wiggled her mouth from side to side. 'Hmm… The thick fur surrounding his face reminds me of a lion cub, so what about… Leo? Like the star sign, Leo the Lion.'

'Sounds perfect!' said Auntie Meg, raising her arms in the air. 'It suits him.'

Hannah's heart filled with love as she

wrapped her arms around him for a cuddle. 'Oh, he's so fluffy.'

Auntie Meg chuckled. 'I'm so pleased you like him. He came from Mr Fisher's cat's litter, and I just simply fell in love with him,' she said, smiling proudly at Leo. 'Come on, I'll show you where your bedroom is.' She dragged Hannah's suitcase up the stairs. 'You might want to unpack whilst I prepare some supper.'

'Thanks, but I'm not feeling hungry,' said Hannah, apologetically. 'We ate a big meal on the train.'

'Oh, OK, love – if, you're sure,' said her auntie kindly. 'Well, I expect you're tired from your journey. Let me know if you need anything.'

'Yeah, I will. Thanks.'

When Auntie Meg left the room, Hannah gently placed Leo on the bed so she could unpack her suitcase. But just as she was about to hang some clothes up in her wardrobe, she couldn't help noticing the bird's-eye view of the sea. Quickly, she shut the curtains and switched the light on, allowing the clothes in her hands to fall onto the floor. The trouble was, she could still hear the waves, smashing against the rocks. *Boom! Boom!* went her heart as she fumbled behind the curtain to shut the window.

'Phew!' she said, now staring at the pile of clothes on the floor and in her suitcase. She wished she'd not brought so many.

After finally squeezing the last outfit into her wardrobe, she tried forcing the door shut, but it had an annoying habit of reopening by itself. 'Oh, well.' She shrugged, deciding to text Mum instead to let her know she'd arrived OK.

Hannah then spent the rest of the evening sending messages back and forth to her best friend, Becky. Time flew, and soon she found herself falling into a deep sleep.

Chapter Three

Peering over the top of her duvet cover, Hannah scanned the bedroom. The morning sun had sneaked through the gap in her curtains, lightening up the lilac walls. For a moment, she'd forgotten where she was… Then she remembered… Cornwall. In Auntie Meg's cottage close to the beach. In fact – it was way too close to the beach.

Forcing herself to get out of bed, Hannah sat on the edge and tried running her fingers through her tangled-up hair as she wondered whether to open the curtains. She knew it would still be there. The sea. It's not like the cottage will have moved overnight or something.

Ignoring her racing heart, she walked steadily on the creaky floor towards the window and took a peek. And there it was. The Sea.

Quickly, she turned towards Leo who was sprawled on top of her bed like a floppy teddy. 'Auntie Meg's not going to be pleased with all those pull marks you've made in the bedding, you know.'

The cute little kitty didn't seem to mind though as his big blue eyes stared sweetly back at her and then he continued digging his claws into the bedding.

'Oh, come here you!' Hannah couldn't resist picking him up for a cuddle.

As he nestled his sleepy head into her arms, she forced herself to look out of the window again. She stared at the honeycomb beach surrounded by rocky cliffs. It was like having their own private beach because there were no pathways to it, except

from the bottom of Auntie Meg's garden. She'd had wooden steps built into the steep slope for access. Bravely, she glanced at the sea, glistening in the golden sunshine as the gentle waves formed bubbles along the seashore. But still, her heart pumped faster, so she stared at the garden instead. At all the different coloured flowers, blanketing together as one. There was even a pink blossom tree, stretching over a wooden bench…

'Hannah, my love!' called her auntie from downstairs.

'Um… yeah.'

'Would you like some breakfast?'

'Yes, please,' said Hannah, just as little Leo leapt out of her arms to follow the smell of food.

'Morning,' said her auntie, tossing pancakes from her frying pan.

'Morning.' Hannah peered over her shoulder. 'Mm… Smells delish.'

Auntie Meg smiled. 'You can take a seat if you like, and I'll serve them up.'

'OK.' Hannah sat down at the dining room table and glanced around the room; it looked very homely with red and cream-checked chair cushions that matched the curtains. Against one wall stood a large oak storage cupboard where antique ornaments were displayed: mostly sea-side ornaments, like dolphins, crabs – and even mermaids.

'So, here we are.' Auntie Meg proudly placed a stack of warm pancakes on the table. Alongside them were dishes of fresh clotted cream, chocolate sauce and mixed berries.

Hannah's stomach rumbled at the smell of them. She could get used to having pancakes for breakfast.

'How are you settling in?' asked Auntie Meg, sitting down beside her. 'Did you sleep well?'

'Yes, thanks,' replied Hannah, helping herself to a delicious-looking pancake. 'I had Leo for company.'

'Ah, that's good.' Auntie Meg stared at Leo as he slurped his cat milk from his dish. 'I think you're both going to get on really well together. I can tell he likes you.'

Hannah smiled. He would definitely help to make her feel better. 'He's gorgeous!'

'Well, it's going to be a lovely day, so you might want to head to the beach and enjoy some sunshine,' suggested Auntie Meg as though it was the best thing ever. 'The sea is calm… and perhaps you could go for a paddle.'

'I'm not going in the sea!' protested Hannah, coughing as a piece of pancake flew out of her mouth.

'OK, that's fine,' said her auntie, raising her hands in the air. 'I'm sorry, I didn't mean to upset you.' She paused and then added, 'Maybe you could just play on the beach then?'

'Don't fancy it.' *How could her auntie even suggest such a thing?* thought Hannah, pushing her pancake around the plate with her fork, then dissecting its middle; it didn't seem appetizing anymore. 'Anyway, I've forgotten my costume.'

'Well, I never!' boomed Auntie Meg. 'You've come all the way to Morvoren, and you haven't brought a cozzy!'

'Um... no.' Hannah felt her cheeks burn like the colour of a tomato.

'Well, that's OK because I've just bought you one.' Springing out of the chair, her auntie dashed into the kitchen to delve into one of her many shopping bags. 'Ta-dah!' She cheered, waving the striped, fluorescent costume in the air.

'Um...' Hannah placed her fork on the plate. After all, it wasn't the pancake's fault. 'Auntie Meg, that's very kind of you, but…'

'But what?'

'I thought Mum had told you.' Hannah's voice wobbled.

'Oh, love.' With a big sigh, her auntie placed the costume over a chair, then sat and placed her warm hand on top of Hannah's. 'Yes, she did. We just thought it would be good for you if you were able to enjoy the seaside again, you know… like you used to. The trouble with fears is they can grow bigger, and that's when they can affect other areas of your life too, like visiting the beach. You used to love playing in the sand.'

'Thanks, but I don't want to go anywhere near the sea.' Hannah wiped her wet nose on her pyjama sleeve.

'OK, love – if, you're sure.' Auntie Meg gave Hannah a warm hug before handing her a tissue. 'Well, if you do change your mind, I could always go with you,' she added, springing to her feet to clear the breakfast pots.

'I'm not gonna change my mind,' mumbled Hannah. She wished her auntie would stop going on about it; it was making her stomach feel funny.

'No worries,' said her auntie from the kitchen sink. 'I suppose you could wear your cozzy in the garden.'

'Yeah, I'd like that,' replied Hannah, feeling her heart settling back into her chest. She knew Auntie Meg had her best interests at heart and wished she could get over her fear… but she didn't know how. A warm tear trickled down her cheek as she stared at the swimming costume and ran her fingers over the sparkly sequins around the heart-shaped pocket. Hmm… She wondered whether to try it on… Just to see what it would look like.

'It's really nice… and sparkly!' exclaimed Hannah, walking into the kitchen as she held the costume at arm's length and admired all the bright colours. 'I think I'll go and try it on.'

Auntie Meg seemed pleased. 'You do that, love – and then come and show me.'

So, Hannah dashed upstairs to try it on. Staring at her reflection in the bedroom mirror, she couldn't help but smile. The costume sparkled and shimmered as she spun and twirled like a ballerina. It looked amazing! Like sooo cool! Maybe she could leave it on whilst doing some bug-hunting in the garden. It was one of her favourite pastimes at home, finding bugs like ladybirds and making them a perfect habitat home.

So, she packed her bag full of really useful stuff and rummaged in the suitcase for her flip-flops. Now, she was all set to explore the garden.

'Wow – look at you!' said Auntie Meg with her arms in the air. 'You look wonderful!'

'Thanks.' Hannah smiled as she gave her a

twirl. 'I do love it.'

Auntie Meg seemed pleased. 'That's good. Now get yourself out there and enjoy some sunshine whilst I give your mum a call – let her know you've settled in OK. Would you like a word with her after?'

'Yeah, can do,' replied Hannah, carrying her bag over her shoulder to venture outside.

Leo followed, squeezing through a small gap in the open door and pitter-pattering into the garden.

'It looks like you've got company. Can you make sure he doesn't stray?'

'Yeah, sure – I'll look after him.' Hannah picked up the cheeky little kitten and strolled along the winding path. A border of pink and white flowers decorated either side until the path split into two. The left path led towards… the sea and there was no way she was going down there. So, she shot off onto the right path, hurrying towards the wooden bench beneath the blossom tree.

After placing Leo on the grass, she plonked her bag on the bench to rummage for her magnifying glass; it came in handy whenever she was bug hunting. 'Ah-ha!' she said, after throwing the contents of her bag onto the bench. 'It's here!'

But when she turned round to show Leo, he'd disappeared. He was chasing a butterfly around the garden. The trouble was… the butterfly fluttered towards the path that led to the beach and Leo scampered after it.

'Hey, Leo!' Throwing the magnifying glass on the bench, she raced after him, sprinting down the steep wooden steps. 'Come back!'

Chapter Four

'Oh, there you are!' said Hannah, panting.

Leo, the picture of innocence, was sprawled out on the sparkly sand, enjoying the morning sun.

'Auntie Meg's not going to be pleased you ran off, you know.'

Leo flashed his huge round eyes at her with a 'Meow!' and flopped his head back onto his legs.

She looked down at him fondly, unable to stay cross with the adorable little kitty. But they couldn't stay here. The waves were spraying into bubbly foam on the seashore and the sea air wafted up her nose. 'C'mon, Leo, let's go!' she said, her stomach feeling funny. 'I'm not hanging around here!'

But as she crouched down to pick him up, the glittery sand covered her hands. She scooped up a big handful. Ahh… The feel of soft sand like tiny jewels running through her tingly fingers. She'd forgotten how much fun it was to play on the beach. She turned her back on the sea and kneeled, gazing at the long stretches of golden sand as if it were the first time she'd seen it…

Soon, she found herself daydreaming about the great time she'd had playing on the beach when she was younger… Building sandcastles, making sand angels, Mum covering her in the sand and sculpting her into a mermaid, and even… even playing in the…

WHOOSH!

Hannah's heart jumped. The gentle waves had now whipped into huge curling waves, roaring and crashing against the rocks. She turned to pick up Leo – but he'd gone. 'Oh, no, Leo!'

He was running towards the sea.

'Come back!' Throwing off her flip-flops, she raced after him. 'Don't go down there!' She had to get to him before he ventured any further.

Luckily, Leo swerved to the right, where there was a tumble of rocks. As Hannah got closer, she realised he had stopped to investigate a rock pool.

'Phew!' she said, gasping for breath. 'Stop running off, you're scare... Wow! Look at all those gold pebbles surrounding the rock pool!' They ran in a rough circle around the edge. Curiously, she knelt and stroked the glossy coating with her fingers. They were as smooth as marble and looked very special.

At that moment, a reddish-brown crab scuttled sideways from behind a gold pebble, and

Leo stretched a paw into the pool to catch it.

'No, Leo, leave it alone.' She gently guided his paw away and the crab crawled back into hiding, tucking its legs and claws in tight.

Still, Leo continued until he got a paw wedged between two of the gold pebbles. 'Meow!'

'Oh, now what have you done?' Quickly, she eased his paw out.

But the cheeky crab scuttled back out again as if it were enjoying the chase, crawling behind one pebble to another – so, Leo climbed on top of a pebble to swipe it.

'C'mon!' she said, trying to pick him up. 'Let's go and play with your toy mouse at home!'

But Leo ignored her. He seemed keen to play, catch the crab, and as hard as she tried, she couldn't budge him; it was as if there was an invisible energy pulling him ever closer to the rock pool. Then the blue sky turned grey, and there was a distant roll of thunder.

'S… something's not right!' Hannah shivered. 'C'mon, Leo, we're going!' She tried grasping hold of him again, her hand shaking – but it was different. The rock pool seemed much deeper – and more threatening. Worse still, the force of the water seemed to be pulling him in.

'Leo! I can't get you!' With all her might, she tried freeing him, but his whole body got dragged into the heart of it. The rock pool had turned into a vicious swirling whirlpool.

'Help!' she yelled. 'Please, someone help!' It was hopeless. There wasn't a single person anywhere. 'Oh, no, this is a nightmare! What's happening now?'

The water was changing colour – reds, yellows, and greens – all the colours of the rainbow. Then there was a gurgling and a glugging sound as the water spun even faster and faster, and little

Leo's helpless body spun around deeper and deeper into the centre of the cruel whirlpool. She had to do something. Fast.

Ignoring the pebbles digging into her stomach, she leaned over and reached in, grabbing hold of his tiny body to pull him out. But she couldn't. The water had sucked him into its powerful grip. Leo's angelic face stared up at her, his eyes wide with terror as he mewled frantic cries and his sodden body squirmed from her grip. And then…

Then he disappeared.

'NO!!!'

Taking a painful breath, she plunged her whole face into the mighty whirlpool, her eyes stinging as she focused on finding Leo. But she couldn't see him. She couldn't see anything. Just a swirling of multi-coloured water flashing past her eyes. With a crazy heartbeat, she jerked her head back out of the water, catching her breath.

What was she going to do now? It was her responsibility to look after him, and no way was she going back to her aunties without him.

But as she forced her head and shoulders into the turbulent whirlpool the water whisked her body around and around like a spider being flushed down the plughole.

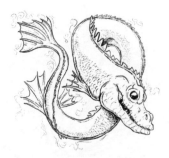

Chapter Five

Hannah's scream got lost as she madly fought with her arms and kicked her legs against the power of the pool. Still, further and further she spiralled as rainbow-coloured water swished past her eyes, spinning and swirling around her helpless body.

Then it went black.

Totally black like a dark hole in the centre of the universe.

That was when Hannah realised… She'd been plunged into the depths of the freezing cold sea.

Belting her way forward, she thrashed her

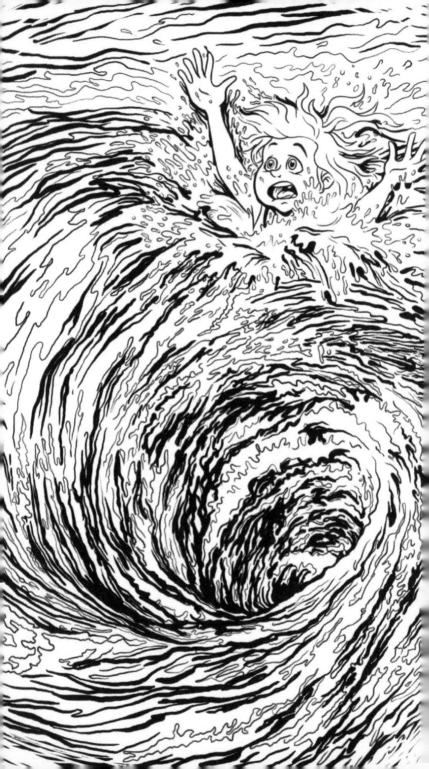

arms and legs, desperate to break the surface – but it was taking forever…

As she passed some brightly coloured fish, she wondered how far down in the terrifying ocean she actually was. She couldn't hold her breath for much longer.

Finally, she coughed and spluttered her way to the surface, gasping for the fresh air to fill her lungs – but where was she? And where was Leo? He was nowhere to be seen.

She kicked her legs and waved her arms in a panic to stay afloat, but the sea spray stung her eyes, and the cruel waves threw her trembling body around; it wasn't easy to see anything let alone try to swim.

Oh, where was Leo? she worried. *He had to be somewhere!*

Then she spotted a tiny white cloud in the distance, being carried away on a surfing wave.

'Leo!' she spluttered, kicking her legs towards him. 'Come back!' But the stormy sea tossed her back again – and poor kitty got smaller and smaller and…

'Le–' she tried shouting, just as another wave rolled over her head.

It was too late.

Leo was gone.

'NO!' yelled Hannah, her voice breaking. 'Please – someone help!' Desperately, she scanned the huge ocean for someone – but it was no use. There was no sign of anyone. No boat. No paraglider. No one.

In the far distance on her left, she could just make out a sliver of white beach. Wondering if Leo had been washed ashore, she immediately headed towards it. She'd got to find the adventurous little kitty no matter what before someone – or something else did.

To her horror, she noticed a pair of bulging red eyes skimming the surface of the sea and glaring straight at her.

Oh no! she panicked. *What's that thing?* It didn't look too friendly.

Despite the cruel waves throwing her back and forth, she flapped her arms madly and kicked her cold, achy legs like a frog towards the beach. But the weird-looking eyes were sneaking ever closer towards her, watching her every move. How would she make it on time? She had no clue, but she'd got to try. If she couldn't save herself, then how could she save poor Leo?

Still, the beach didn't seem to be getting any closer and as she dared to glance round, the red bulging eyes were almost upon her. At the same time, she spotted a grey fin slicing through the sea and heading straight towards her. Oh, no! This was it! She was gonna die. If the monstrous eyes didn't

kill her, the shark definitely would!

Quickly, she spun in the opposite direction –
belting her arms and legs forwards as she spat out
the salty seawater that got in her –

'Aaaaargh!' Hannah's cold, shivering body
was swooped up and carried by a…

'Ee-Ee-Ee-Ee-Ee-Ee.'

A… A dolphin. She allowed herself to
breathe again as a huge sigh of relief washed over
her. She was alive. The shark wasn't a shark after
all, but a beautiful dolphin. And, with a click and a
whistle, he sped off through the sea.

'Whoa!' Hannah clung onto the dolphin's
soft, rubbery fin, leaning forward to keep her
balance as he sliced through the waves faster than a
jet ski.

But were the sneaky eyes still following
them? She glanced over her shoulder to see.

Far behind them was a black monstrous head

in the water, allowing her to catch a glimpse of its scariness before the dolphin dived again. It seemed the sea monster was still giving chase.

With a shiver, her white knuckles clung even tighter to the dolphin's fin, water streaming through her hair as she took a deep breath when the dolphin leapt and held her breath when he dived into a wave. Now wasn't a good time to fall into the choppy waters.

The dolphin was unstoppable – whooshing through the sea and making whistling sounds like a twittering bird. Had the monster kept the same speed?

She looked all around her but couldn't see it anywhere.

Breathing a sigh of relief, she realised how lucky she had been to be rescued by the graceful dolphin. Although it wasn't easy riding on the dolphin's back. She tried moving her body in sync with him as he swerved this way and then that, up and over the oncoming waves. One slip of her hand and she'd be straight back in the water again, so she kept holding tight around his fin, using her precious time to look for Leo as they continued propelling through the ocean.

But where were they going? And where was Leo? Was he still alive? Her heart grew heavy, and her stomach swirled with worry. She desperately needed to find him. Auntie Meg had trusted her to look after him and she couldn't fail.

Chapter Six

The storm passed and silver clouds floated away to leave a blanket of pale blue sky. The dolphin swooshed through the ocean as though on a mission – but where to? She hadn't a clue. Then it became apparent. He was heading straight towards an object in the sea that looked like a huge rock.

As they got much closer, Hannah realised it wasn't a sea rock at all, but a giant pearl, glistening in the sun. She'd never seen anything like it before! It was marbled with different shades of pink – and so bright and shiny!

Suddenly, the dolphin stopped, raising his

body and snout high above the water, towards the sky.

'Whoa!' Hannah felt as though she was riding a bucking bronco as the dolphin dived once more, causing her to cough from another drenching. She scooped her hair from her face; it felt like wet, tangled seaweed.

With a squawk and a squeak, her riding partner whistled at a girl sitting on the dome-shaped pearl. At first glance, Hannah thought she was a girl. A human girl about the same age as herself. But she'd got a tail. A bright turquoise-blue tail that she flipped from side to side.

Surely, she wasn't a mermaid. She couldn't be... Could she? Mermaids didn't exist... Did they?

Hannah screwed her eyes shut in disbelief and then reopened them. Wow! Her petite freckled face was still there! And she still looked... She still looked very much like a mermaid with the most

amazing long rainbow-coloured hair that she seemed to be enjoying plaiting.

Realising she was being totally uncool; Hannah forced her mouth shut and glanced away. Instead, she focused on keeping her balance as the fidgety dolphin rocked from side to side like a boat, flapping his flippers excitedly at the mermaid.

When Hannah did glance back, the girl was staring straight back at her. In fact, it was more than a stare; it was more like a scowl really. *Oh great,* she thought. *The dolphin has brought me here to meet an unfriendly mermaid... But why? Hmm... Mum had always said, "Don't judge people until you get to know them." Maybe she's just a little unsure – like me.* So, Hannah made the effort to smile, letting her know she was friendly.

Still, the hair-obsessed girl continued to scowl at her whilst messing with her plait. Hannah wondered why she was bothering. It seemed clear she didn't want to be friends. *Oh, the sooner I find Leo, the better. Then we can get out of this weird place.*

At that moment, the mermaid slid down the huge pearl with her arms in the air, splashing gently into the sea. 'Hey there, Domitius, and…?' She tilted her head to one side, narrowing her watery blue eyes at Hannah as though she didn't trust her.

'Hi, I'm Hannah.' She gave a quick wave then continued holding on tight to Domitius's fin.

'Ah, OK,' was all the mermaid could say before kissing Domitius's snout. Then, with a flick of her tail, she sped off through the sea.

'Hey, there!' Hannah shouted. 'Do you have a n-a-a-a-a-m-e?' Her voice wobbled as Domitius split the ocean in half with his beak to catch up with the sea girl.

'Of course I have a name!' snapped the mermaid, now rippling through the sea beside her.

'It's Marcella!' she said proudly. 'But you can call me Marcie.'

'OK, sure!' replied Hannah as Domitius glided through the calmer waves with an 'Ee-Ee-Ee-Ee' sound in her ear. 'Um, where are we going?'

'To see Neptune, of course.'

'Neptune!' said Hannah in disbelief. She wasn't sure mermaids existed until now let alone some sea god. 'I don't want to see Neptune!' She wanted to find Leo. Desperately. She scanned the ocean for the little kitty, straining her eyes to see as far as she could. But it was no use; he was nowhere to be seen. Still, she had to keep hoping she'd find him and that he was OK. Maybe Neptune could help? 'Why are we going to see Neptune anyway?'

'We've been summoned to take you to Neptune's cave,' said Marcie as though Hannah had done something terrible. 'After all, you have just entered his kingdom.'

'I'm sorry, there's been some mistake.'
Hannah's eyes brimmed with tears, making it
difficult for her to see. 'I need to find Leo so we can
go back home to Auntie Meg's. He's disappeared in
the sea.'

'Oh!' Marcie seemed surprised. 'Who's Leo?
I didn't realise someone else had entered our world
too.'

'He's a white fluffy, adorably cute little
kitten with the bluest…' Hannah's voice wobbled,
and she couldn't continue as tears streamed down
her cheeks, mixing with the salty splashes of the
sea.

'Ah – OK. He sounds sweet,' said Marcie,
showing some sympathy. 'Well, I hope you find
him because Neptune will probably want to see you
both.'

'Yeah, thanks. I hope I find him too.'
Hannah's head pounded with worry, praying he was

still alive. Maybe he'd managed to scramble onto some rocks… or even made it to the seashore. She stared towards the crescent-shaped beach which was now much closer in view. The sand was the whitest she'd ever seen, like glistening frost on a winter's morning. Staring at the turquoise-blue sea all around, Hannah kept hoping she'd find little Leo.

'Where does your auntie live?' Marcie sounded curious as to where Hannah had come from.

'Um.' Hannah stared over at the left side of the beach looking for a cottage nestled on a cliff, but as she'd already feared, this wasn't Morvoren. All she could see beyond the beach was hill after hill in various shades of green and what looked like some houses nestled in a small village. 'My auntie's cottage was over there in that direction.' She pointed to the left side of the beach, keeping one hand firmly gripped on Domitius's fin. 'But it's not there anymore and that's not Morvoren Beach.' Her heart deflated like a popped balloon.

'Well, of course it's not Morvoren Beach, wherever that is. It's Neptune's Beach, and when you've sorted this mess out that you've got us all in, you'll be able to go back home.'

'What mess? What are you talking about?'

But Marcie didn't answer. Instead, she began singing *totally* out of tune.

Oh, that sea-girl is so annoying! thought Hannah as Domitius whizzed her through the sea. *The sooner I get out of here, the better.*

'Just so you know,' began Marcie, interrupting her own singing.

Hannah groaned.

'Neptune is the ruler of the sea world, and he takes great pride in looking after it – and he knows when people have entered his kingdom.'

'OK, sea-girl, I'm not sure what you're

trying to say, but I didn't ask for any of this. To be whisked off into this unfriendly place.'

'Hey, we are not unfriendly!'

'Yeah… course not. Well, as soon as I've found Leo, we'll be out of here!'

But Marcie just ignored her to sing another screechy tune.

'Anyway, where is Neptune's cave?' Hannah bellowed over the top of Marcie's singing, but still she continued a while before replying.

'It's situated underneath those rocks.' She pointed to the right side of the beach where they were heading. 'It looks like a huge rock from where we are, but Neptune had it built that way.'

'Why?'

'Because he wanted it as his hideout, you know. He didn't want his enemies to know about it.'

'Enemies!'

'Uh-huh.'

Hannah wondered what sort of enemies. He certainly sounded very protective of his kingdom.

Chapter Seven

As they got closer to Neptune's cave, Hannah noticed there were two entrances: one over the sea and one beside the beach. Domitius headed towards the cut-out rock over the sea that had been made into an archway.

Hmm... she thought. *I hope it's more homely inside. It looks dark and gloomy from the outside.*

And with a swoosh, Domitius swam under the arch, making high-pitched whistling noises along the way.

'Domitius is informing Neptune of our arrival,' explained Marcie, speeding ahead of them.

'Ah, OK.' Hannah shuddered, wondering what Neptune would be like as Domitius stopped at the water's edge.

Then with a flick of his tail, Domitius leapt into the air towards the stalactites dangling up above.

'Whoa!' Hannah's hand slipped from Domitius's fin, and she nearly fell back into the sea. Quickly, she grabbed hold to steady herself before climbing onto the rock bed.

So, this must be Hannah's stop. With a shudder, she looked all around. A red rug lay in the middle of the cave floor, but it didn't look very homely. The walls were drenched in water and there were cracks in the ground.

'Thank you, Domitius!' said Neptune, making Hannah jump as his deep voice echoed all around the cave.

'Th-thanks, Domitius.' Hannah crouched

down to kiss his soft, velvety skin at the water's edge and Marcie gave him a gentle stroke.

He responded with a flap of his flippers and an 'Ee-Ee-Ee-Ee' before gliding out of the cave.

But Marcie didn't look as though she was going anywhere. She was now cupping her face in her hands as she rested her elbows on the edge of the rock bed.

Hannah slowly turned around to see a large figure in the far corner of the cave; his shadow almost touched the stalactites that dangled dangerously from the roof.

With just a few giant steps, he strode towards her.

She gulped. *Was this really Neptune?* A gold crown nestled on top of his white, curly hair, which fell disobediently around his face, merging with his messy moustache and long beard. A cream robe draped loosely around his huge, sturdy body, and in one hand he grasped his gold trident; Hannah wondered what the brightly coloured buttons on the handle were used for. They looked like sparkly gems.

Neptune's sea-coloured eyes glared down at her. 'Now then, Hannah!' he boomed, his huge body towering above her.

Hannah's throat tightened. How did he know her name? And hang on a min– Who's that? Nestled in Neptune's robes, swishing his white fluffy tail from side to side was...

'Hey, Leo!' she said, elatedly.

Leo jumped down from a mighty height and pitter-pattered towards Hannah, his huge innocent eyes looking up at her as though he wondered where she had been.

'Oh, Leo, I thought I'd lost you!' She picked him up and drew him close, hugging him tight. 'Well, you're here with me now, so we can –'

'Please!' Neptune placed his burgundy velvet footstool on the rug. 'Sit down. I've been expecting you.'

Thump! Thump! went her heart! She felt sure he could hear it.

Like a king on the throne, he sat down on a golden chair that looked very grand with a burgundy velvet seat. Beside his chair was a large rock pool in which numerous kinds of coloured fish were splashing in and out of the water.

'You can't go home until you've solved the code,' said Neptune, his eyes boring into hers.

'W-wait – what!' Hannah stared up at him in disbelief.

'When you entered my kingdom, you dislodged a gold pebble that was part of a protection circle defending my rock pool from negative forces.'

'I don't understand!'

'Hundreds of years ago, we had a plague of sea monsters killing innocent sea creatures. I had to save my sea world from being infested by them, so I cast a spell. Some monsters died and the others retreated into the depths of the ocean, falling into a deep sleep,' he went on. 'Then I placed some magic pebbles around my rock pool to protect my kingdom from negativity. The pebbles form a magic circle; an invisible layer of protection – meaning they only allow good energy to enter. But now, Hannah, now – the spell has been broken and all its power lost!'

'But why?'

'Because you broke the spell when you disturbed the inscribed gold pebble, allowing your fears to enter my kingdom. All the gold pebbles around my rock pool were protecting my kingdom with positivity, love, and happiness. And now that a gold pebble has left the circle, the rock pool is open to negative forces again.'

'Oh, no!' said Hannah, her hands covering her mouth. 'You mean the shiny pebbles? I'm sorry – it was Leo. He disappeared and –'

'Your thoughts are energy, and they are very powerful,' interrupted Neptune. 'You attract circumstances into your life by what you think about – good or bad. And your fearful thoughts of sea monsters have given them their life back causing them to resurface, so now the sea world is in danger again because the monsters are feeding off your fear!'

'How can my thoughts attract stuff into my life?'

'Now, because you're the one who's broken the spell, you're the one who has to solve the code!' he said, completely ignoring her question.

'But, Neptune, please, we just want to go home!' Her voice wobbled as a warm tear trickled down her cold cheek. 'My Auntie Meg will be wondering where we are.'

Still, he said, 'I don't have the power to send you home until you've solved the code and saved my sea world from destruction.'

'And how can I do that?'

'You must find the inscribed gold pebble that you displaced upon entering my kingdom and solve the inscription on it. When you have solved the code, the sea world will be at peace again, and then – and only then – you will be able to return home.'

Hannah stared at little Leo; his soft, fluffy body laying comfy on her lap. If she had to solve the code before they could return home, then that's what she'd do. It couldn't be that difficult. 'OK, so where is this gold pebble?'

'You're the one who's removed it, so you're the one who has to find it.'

'But –'

'Try to understand this!' bellowed Neptune.

Leo let out a scared 'meow,' jumping down from Hannah's knee and hiding beneath the stool.

Suddenly, the cave began to tremble, and mighty waves flooded the ground.

'They're here!' proclaimed Neptune, rising to his giant feet.

'Who?' Hannah jumped up from the chair, looking all around. 'Who's here?'

Chapter Eight

'It's the sea monsters, Hannah,' said Marcie, gripping the rock's surface. 'They're all waking up from the bottom of the ocean!'

'Oh!' Hannah picked up Leo from beneath the chair; she couldn't bear to lose him again.

'We must prepare for battle!' roared Neptune, banging his trident on the rock bed.

'W-we?' said Hannah in disbelief. This had nothing to do with solving a code. The whole situation just seemed to be getting worse.

Just then, a colossal wave swooped over Marcie's head, so she leapt out of the water and onto the rock bed just as Neptune pressed a bright blue gem on his trident.

'Wow, that's so cool!' gasped Hannah, staring in amazement. The blast of air shooting out of the trident's three prongs flushed the rushing waves back into the sea.

'Here, take my trident!' ordered Neptune, even though it was twice the size of Hannah.

'Wh-What?' she stuttered. 'Why?'

'I have to go now and help Domitius protect our kingdom.'

'But what about Leo?' Hannah stared at his tiny body in her arms. She couldn't believe this was happening. She couldn't believe she was in such a terrifying place.

'He will be fine on my chair.' Neptune pointed to his chair and then firmly held out the trident once more; he wasn't going to take no for an answer.

'Umm.' Hannah wasn't so sure Leo would be fine but found herself saying, 'OK' anyway. After giving Leo one last stroke, she reluctantly placed him on Neptune's chair and took hold of the trident. 'Whoa!' she cried, nearly falling backwards onto the soggy rug. 'It's huge – and heavy!'

'Bye for now!' Neptune's huge figure strode purposefully towards the sea.

'No – wait!'

'The trident will help whilst you learn how to solve the code!' And without even a backward glance, he dived beneath the sea at lightning speed.

Now what was she supposed to do? He'd left her to defend the cave with a weapon she could barely hold, let alone know how to use.

Harsh winds blasted through the cave, now whipping the waves into a frenzy as they smashed against the surface edge and onto the rock bed.

Staring at all the brightly coloured gems on

the handle, Hannah wondered which one to press. There was a bright blue one, a sparkling white, a plum, and even a silvery moon colour. Oh, which one should she use?

Remembering what Neptune had done, she pressed the blue gem and directed the fork end of the trident towards the waves but, like a super-fast hairdryer, the trident seemed to have a mind of its own, and a blast of air styled Leo's tufty head instead.

He stared innocently up at her with a 'Meow' as if to say, 'What are you doing to me?'

'Oops, sorry!' said Hannah, just as a monstrous noise grew louder and louder. Slowly, she turned her head and shivered. A dark eerie shadow lurked beneath the water that ran alongside the rock bed. 'I… um… think we've got company.'

'Use the trident!' yelled Marcie from the rock pool.

'Uh huh!' Hannah responded. She knew she'd got to protect them all and use the trident, but she was struggling to keep hold; it was as if she'd lost the use of her body.

Then, just like a noisy boat coming into shore, the black shadow groaned and reared its monstrous black head out of the water with a thunderous 'ROAR!' all around the cave.

'Aaaaaaaargh!' The trident slipped from Hannah's fingers, dropping to the flooded ground with a splash. 'It's a-a sea monster!'

As the hideous thing scanned the cave for something, anything to attack, its swirling, red eyes spotted Hannah – then with an evil grin, licked its razor-sharp teeth.

She wanted to run, but her knees were trembling, and her feet wouldn't budge. She tried shouting for help, but no words would come out.

'Come on, Hannah – before it's too late!'

screeched Marcie as she somersaulted out of the rock pool.

'Um. Yeah. Right, OK.' Swallowing a fearful breath, Hannah wrapped her shaky hands around the wet trident once more. 'You s-stay there, I've got it!'

'Well quick then!'

'Yeah, yeah.' As Hannah's legs swayed in the rising water, she pointed the trident at the sea monster, pressing the blue button to fire freezing cold air into its crazy-looking eyes.

With an ear-piercing noise, the monster's eyes shut but then flickered open again, looming its ginormous head over her.

'NO!' she cried, falling backwards into the water.

'Meow!' Poor Leo seemed terrified as he leapt down from Neptune's chair to hide behind it.

He needed her. Marcie needed her. This was

her duty. So, she scrambled in the water and rose to her trembling feet. But where was the trident?

'Go on!' yelled Marcie to the monster, now sitting on the flooded rug shooting frosty air into the monster's eyes with the trident. 'Beat it!'

And with a loud shrieking noise, the horrid thing spun its head around and around and around.

Hannah covered her eyes with her hands, still peeking through the gaps of her fingers as Marcie continued using the trident like a gun.

Still spinning its head with a deafening shrieking sound, the monster slowly retreated into the depths of the ocean. And at the same time, the stormy waves settled, flushing back into the sea.

'Hah!' said Marcie, flicking her fluke back and forth as though she was really proud of herself. 'That worked!'

'Yeah, thanks.' Hannah quickly picked up the trident before she snatched it off her again. 'But

I said I'd got it.'

'No, you hadn't!' snapped the bossy mermaid as she tossed her plait over her shoulder. 'You were too scared. You couldn't even control the trident from shaking so much.'

'No, I wasn't!' objected Hannah, despite her still trembling. Placing the trident beside Neptune's chair, she picked up Leo to kiss his cute pink nose. He may not have needed a cuddle, but she did.

'We can't let the sea monsters win, you know,' said Marcie, somersaulting towards the rock pool again.

Hannah sighed. 'Yeah, I know,' she said, although all she cared about at that moment was tucking her head in close to Leo's and holding him tight.

But then he jumped to the ground, favouring the rock pool to a hug.

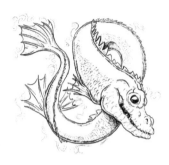

Chapter Nine

'Leo, come away from the rock pool!' said Hannah, darting towards him in a panic.

But curious little Leo ignored her to paw at an innocent crab creeping out from behind a gold pebble. Luckily, the clever crab outsmarted his attempts by scuttling past back and forth, back and forth.

'No, Leo, not again!' She gently grabbed hold of him, placing him down beside her with a reassuring stroke. 'Leave the crab alone. We don't want you disappearing again.'

The picture of cuteness stared up at her with

a 'meow' and then flopped his head onto his legs.

'How strange,' said Hannah.

'What is?' asked Marcie, re-plaiting her hair and tying it with some seaweed.

'The gold pebbles surrounding this rock pool – they look very similar to the pebbles on Morvoren beach.'

'The one on… erm… whatever beach you just said, must be one of Neptune's rock pools.'

'Neptune's?' said Hannah, puzzled.

'Yep,' confirmed Marcie, as she continued plaiting her hair as if it was the most important thing in the world. 'All Neptune's rock pools are surrounded by gold pebbles.'

'Well, I hope there's a better way home!' Hannah couldn't bear the thought of being whisked into another whirlpool. 'And that crab…' The crab was now staring up at her as though it understood what she was saying. 'It looks similar to the one Leo chased on Morvoren beach.'

'Te-he!' Marcie laughed. 'Neptune must have rescued Cardea from there. She is a very adventurous crab.'

As Cardea scuttled behind yet another gold pebble, Hannah noticed an inscription on it. 'Do you know what that says?' She ran her finger under the inscription.

'Ooh – interesting!' exclaimed Marcie, lowering her head to see. 'How peculiar!'

'What, the pebble?'

'No – the inscription! I've never seen it before. Maybe it has something to do with Neptune's secret code, but I don't know what it says – it's too small to read.'

'Hmm…' Hannah took a closer look to read but it was way too small. 'So how can we find out what it says?'

'I've got just the thing.'

'Have you?'

'Yep, my magnifying glass.'

'Brilliant idea!' Hannah scanned the cave but couldn't see it lying around anywhere. 'Where is it?'

'It's in my castle.'

'Your castle! Where's that?'

'Ooh, about a mile past my giant sea pearl where we met.'

'Wait – what?' screeched Hannah. 'But that's in the sea!'

'It sure is.' Marcie grinned excitedly as though it would be fun. 'Come on, let's go and get it. I'll show you, my slide.'

'Um… I'm OK, thanks, I'm not a slide person. Not ones in the middle of the sea anyhow.'

'Ah, don't be daft!' Marcie went on. 'Wait till you see it – you'll love it.'

Hannah's stomach churned just thinking

about Marcie's slide. 'No, Marcie, I won't! I won't love it at all!' She quickly wiped her eyes dry before a tear leaked. 'How about I stay here and guard the cave with Leo whilst you go and fetch it – and then I can read the inscription.'

Marcie giggled as though Hannah had said a joke. 'No, no, no, no, no! You're coming with me!' she said, climbing out of the rock pool and wetting Hannah through. 'It's your code to solve – I'm not doing all the work for you.' And with a roly-poly to the water's edge, she flipped herself forward into the sea with a splash.

Good thing she did too, because at that moment, Hannah felt like booting her in there. Anyway, she had no intention of joining her. Her tummy still felt funny, and she'd now got a headache. Maybe she wasn't very well which meant she ought to rest. That's what she'd do at home. So, she sat beside Leo and tucked her quivering legs into her body, wrapping her arms securely around them. 'I'm sorry – I can't go back in there again.'

'Can't or won't?'

'I don't feel very well,' said Hannah, her whole-body shivering.

'Oh, come on, Hannah!' said Marcie, impatiently.

Hannah ignored her. She wouldn't understand anyway. No one did.

'Is it the sea monsters?'

'Sea monsters? No. Well. Yes, a little, I guess. It's just that…'

'What? What is it?' Showing some sympathy, Marcie rested her elbows on the rock bed to listen.

Hannah edged closer to Marcie, shuffling forwards on her bottom as though she'd lost the use of her legs, then stopped to sit on Neptune's wet rug. 'I... I… can't swim,' she stuttered. 'And… I…

I'm terrified of the water.' The words tumbled out of her mouth as she released a painful breath.

'Oh.' Marcie stared at her as though it was the weirdest thing she'd ever heard. 'Well, how about I teach you?'

'Um, no thanks,' said Hannah. Marcie seemed to have an answer for everything.

'I'm an excellent swimmer, and I know this ocean like the back of my webbed tail!' Marcie swished her tail from side to side to demonstrate.

'I… I really don't think I can,' began Hannah, clearing her throat. 'When I was five years old, I nearly drowned in the sea on Morvoren Beach. Mum and Dad were sunbathing at the time, so I decided to have a paddle.' She paused, recalling the horrific accident. 'Mum told me to stay where my feet could touch the sandy bottom, but then they started talking to each other, so I decided to venture further. Then suddenly… Suddenly, I found myself being dragged underwater by a monstrous sea creature. I thrashed my arms and legs around to be freed, but its sharp teeth gnawed into my ankle. The pain was unbearable like an intense burning sensation as though my ankle and foot were on fire. I was petrified! I thought I was going to die. Anyway, I can't remember much after that. Except waking up on a sunbed with Mum crying as she pressed on my chest to resuscitate me. She said they'd noticed I'd disappeared and had rescued me just in time, although another split second and it would have been too late.'

Marcie gasped in surprise. 'It must have been so scary!'

'Yeah… It was.'

'Did they see the little fish that bit you?'

'It wasn't a little fish, OK.' Hannah lifted her leg to show Marcie the bite scar, which was shaped in a rough circle surrounding her ankle.

Marcie leaned over the rock bed to take a closer look. 'Oooh!' She flinched. 'That's some scar! You had a very lucky escape.'

'Anyway, apparently, they never saw what attacked me; it must have swum away. But I did! I did see it – and I'm telling you it was HUGE!'

'OK, OK! So, I'm guessing you haven't been in the water since?'

'Nope. Not until today.'

'But you can do this, Hannah. I'll be with you every stroke of the way, I promise.'

Chapter Ten

Hannah knew in her heart that she ought to join
Marcie. After all, Neptune said she'd got to solve
the code and save the sea world from destruction.
But more importantly than that was precious Leo,
who trusted her to get him home safely. And maybe.
Just maybe. She'd have to swim to be able to do
that. She had to do it. It was now or never! So,
despite her heart banging against her chest, she took
a deep breath and said, 'OK, I'll do it.'

'Great!' cheered Marcie, as though it were
the easiest thing in the world.

Hannah stared at little Leo, now curled up on

Neptune's seat. 'Will he be safe if I leave him here?'

'Yep, of course. No harm can come to him while he's on the throne.'

'Well, I hope you're right.' Hannah's legs wobbled as she forced herself to get up off the wet rug. 'You stay here, little one and guard the cave, OK.'

Leo flickered his eyes open at her as he continued resting his sleepy head on his legs.

'Hmm.' She kissed the top of his fluffy head. 'It doesn't look as though you've got any intentions of going anywhere.'

Slowly, she wandered towards the water. It seemed calm enough apart from Marcie performing a front-flip here and a backflip there as though the sea were fun.

A cold shudder ran through her body as she slumped down at the edge of the rock bed and dangled her legs in the water. *C'mon Hannah, get it together. You can do this.* She told herself. *You've fought the treacherous waves and rode all the way here on Domitius's back. Surely, you can learn to swim and help save Neptune's Kingdom.* 'Brrr, it's cold!' she splashed water onto her legs.

'Oh, you'll soon warm up,' encouraged Marcie, beckoning her forwards. 'Come on in, I'll teach you how to swim.'

'Alright, here goes.' Hannah eased herself into the water, kicking her arms and legs frantically to stay afloat, but then she spluttered from swallowing some water.

'Wait – where are you going?'

'I'm getting out,' spluttered Hannah, clambering back onto the side.

'Hey, you've got to do this sooner rather than later. Neptune needs our help before the sea monsters take over his kingdom.'

Hannah shuddered. The thought of scary monsters slithering in the sea was freaking her out.

'Come on,' Marcie went on. 'We'll stay close to the seashore whilst you learn how to swim.'

'D'you promise?'

'Yep, I promise.'

So once again Hannah took a deep breath and slid back in, doggy-paddling to stay afloat until Marcie took hold of her hand and guided her out of the cave.

'So, kick your legs behind you,' instructed Marcie as she flipped her tail fin up and down. 'Glide for a bit and pull yourself forward with your arms before pushing the water away, like this.'

Hannah continued doggy paddling as she observed Marcie gracefully rippling through the sea. She so wished she could swim like that.

'OK, did you get it?' asked Marcie, spinning around to watch her copy.

'Get it? Erm…' Marcie made it look like the easiest thing in the world, like when Mr Numerius was explaining maths. 'I think so, but it's not easy. I feel like I'm gonna drown.'

'You won't drown! You're doing erm…' Marcie sounded concerned as she watched Hannah's swimming attempt. 'Erm… Yep, you're doing OK… I guess.'

'No, I'm not though, am I?' Hannah's heart raced as she thought about making a quick exit towards the beach.

'You'll be fine. Just keep practising.'

So, she did. She copied Marcie back and forth along the seashore; making sure she tilted her head back as far out of the water as possible.

'OK, you look like you're swimming fine to me now,' said Marcie, showing off with a double backflip in the air. 'Do you think you're ready to swim to my castle?'

Hannah paused, then swallowed a fearful breath. 'I… erm… I guess so.'

'Come on then – follow me!' said Marcie, seemingly enjoying the adventure. 'We're heading over in that direction.' She pointed towards her castle, but all Hannah could see was the endless blue ocean, sparkling in the sun like millions and trillions of tiny diamonds. And to her left, was Marcie's huge sea pearl where they'd first met.

As they began their journey towards the castle, Marcie began to sing again. Hannah tried looking at the positive side, just like her mum had always said. But the only good thing she could think of was that her voice might be keeping away any monsters lurking beneath the water…

Only then she felt various-sized fish swimming in different directions all around her, through her legs and whooshing past her toes. She was sure they were just harmless fish. Harmless fish

doing their own thing. But then one bumped into her ankle, so she swam faster, gaining enough momentum to catch up with the wannabe pop star.

'Hey there!' Marcie looked surprised to see Hannah swimming beside her.

'Hi,' said Hannah, panting. She felt very proud of her newfound swimming achievement. It was a shame she couldn't receive a swimming certificate for all her effort: *Congratulations to Hannah for being a Top Swimmer!* That would be so awe—

There was a loud groan from behind them, much louder than Marcie's singing. As Hannah dared peer over her shoulder, she spotted something in the distance, sneakily following their trail. Even from afar, she could see its red bulging eyes spying the surface of the sea. It looked like trouble, and she wasn't hanging around to find out.

'Um…' She patted Marcie's arm. 'Th-there's

a sea monster chasing us. We're not gonna make it.'

'Oh, it's probably just an innocent fish or something,' said Marcie, continuing to sing as she bobbed up and down in unison with the waves.

'Or something!' shrieked Hannah, giving her a nudge to turn round.

Marcie turned her head. 'Uh-oh! It's a sea monster!'

'Oh no!' cried Hannah. 'Where're Neptune and Domitius?'

'We're nearly there! Just keep your speed up and we can make it!'

Hannah peeked over her shoulder again. 'Oh, flip!'

The monster's eyes glared into hers as it sneaked ever closer towards them.

'It's coming!'

'Just keep swimming!' urged Marcie, seemingly scared herself.

Still, Hannah couldn't help but glance round. Her heart hammered in fright to see the monster had now raised its giant head out of the water and was showing off its huge dinosaur-like teeth, ready to attack! She kicked her legs furiously, trying to find the energy to keep pelting forward.

Chapter Eleven

'Come on, Hannah – keep going!' encouraged Marcie. 'We're nearly at my castle now.'

And there in the distance was Marcie's crystal blue castle magnificently rising above the sea. Although Hannah struggled to enjoy its beauty as her thoughts were still on the deathly monster sneaking behind. Bravely, she turned her head once more to check its whereabouts, but she couldn't see it anywhere.

'Where's it gone?' she asked Marcie, wondering if it was hiding somewhere – waiting for its opportunity to pounce.

'What?'

'The sea monster!' Hannah looked all around as far as she could see. 'It was there a moment ago and now it's gone!'

'Oh, they don't like our castle.'

'Really, why not?'

'The fluorescent blue light blinds their eyes,' said Marcie, grinning. 'So my mum says anyway.'

Hannah breathed a sigh of relief. 'Ah, OK... So, are we safe for now? Here – at your castle?'

'Yep.'

'That's good.' Hannah panted. 'Because I don't think I can swim much further.' Still, she found some energy to propel herself towards the castle.

Marcie swam ahead, gliding towards the entrance steps, which were partially situated beneath the sea. Then with a flick of her tail, she somersaulted up them and gracefully sat down in front of an archway decorated with flowers on either side. 'Come on!'

'Yeah, I'm coming,' said Hannah, allowing her breath to return to normal as she passed some clownfish swimming in circles of silver and red. 'We're not all as quick as you.'

Finally, she reached the stunning castle, glad to be resting her tired legs on the first crystal step above the sea.

'You, OK?' asked Marcie with a puzzled look on her face. She just didn't seem to understand how tired Hannah was from swimming such a distance.

'Yeah. I just need five minutes, that's all.'

'Sure,' said Marcie, even though she was stroking her plait over and over and flipping her tail back and forth impatiently.

Hannah gasped in amazement at the bright blue castle sparkling and glistening in the warm sunshine. It looked like an enormous bright blue gem that had been carved into the shape of a castle with four shiny turrets almost touching the blue sky. Beyond the archway was a castle-shaped door with multi-coloured flowers surrounding it.

'Your castle is awesome!' she said. 'I didn't know castles like this existed.'

'Thanks,' said Marcie, beaming with pride. 'I live with my mum and dad.'

'It's *so* cool!'

Marcie laughed. 'Mum says it's very ancient. If you climb those spiral steps to the right, they circle all around the castle and take you to the very top.'

'Really!' Hannah shielded her eyes from the sun to see; it looked incredible, but she'd much prefer a castle on land.

'You like it, right?' Marcie tilted her head to one side.

'Erm… yeah… but –'

'Well, when we've climbed to the top, we can whizz back down on my super-shiny slide over there.' Marcie's petite finger pointed to an almost vertical slide on their left. 'It takes you straight back into –'

'Whoa – wait!' Hannah's stomach spun. It was the biggest slide she'd ever seen, stopping just a few inches from the sea for maximum splash factor. 'I'm sorry – but no! It looks great fun and all… That is, if it were in a park somewhere, but not in the middle of the sea.'

'Hey, this is your journey as much as mine!' Marcie folded her arms in a sulk. 'Look – my magnifying glass is right at the very top, and you're coming with me to collect it.'

Hannah stayed silent. Marcie just didn't understand.

'Hannah…' began Marcie.

'What?'

'I need you to do this for me... Please,' pleaded Marcie.

'I… I'm not sure.'

'You're swimming great now, and it'll help you overcome your fear.'

Hannah stared all around at the vast ocean as far as her eyes could see, but there was nothing. Nothing visible, anyhow. 'Are you sure there are no sea monsters close by?'

'Yep, I'm sure as the fluke on my tail,' said Marcie, now twirling her plait around her finger.

Hannah stared at the slide… feeling sick just looking at it. Still, she knew the mermaid wasn't going anywhere without her. Maybe Neptune had told Marcie to keep an eye on her. Just in case she escaped. Hah. Fat chance of that. There was nowhere to escape to. So, ignoring her swirling stomach, she dragged her tired achy legs up off the step and found herself saying, 'C'mon then, lead the way.'

'Great!' said Marcie, her huge grin puffing out her freckly cheeks. 'Follow me.' Using her tail, she jumped up onto the step and continued through the archway.

Hannah followed, carefully watching where she was stepping so as not to slip. 'How can you walk on the end of your tail?' she asked, watching Marcie fly up the steps with ease. 'It looks so delicate.'

'My fluke is stronger than it looks.' Marcie jumped in the air to demonstrate, skipping a few steps along the way. 'My all-time favourite though is somersaults.'

'Ah, OK, now you're just showing off again!'

'Hey, I could teach you.'

'What – how to show off?'

'No, silly! How to do somersaults.'

'I'm good thanks, I've only just learnt how to swim,' Hannah nervously followed her onto the first curved step surrounding the castle as Marcie continued somersaulting like an acrobat. 'Don't fall on top of me. I might end up in the sea, and it's beginning to look like quite a drop.'

'Te-he! I've been somersaulting up these steps for as long as I can remember and not had one accident yet.'

'Yet!'

Finally, they reached the top of the castle. Hannah's legs wobbled as she glanced back at the steep, curved steps she had climbed, steeper than any castle she'd ever visited.

'Hey, come over here,' beckoned Marcie, leaning over a balcony.

Hannah grabbed hold of the curved balustrade to steady herself; it reminded her of the balconies at the theatre. 'Wow!' She had to admit, it looked really cool as she gazed over the top at the huge ocean beneath. The sunlight was streaming down on Neptune's Kingdom, dancing across the waves and showing different shades of blue. Far in the distance was a thin white line of beach and to the left was the small village she'd spotted earlier surrounded by hills and mountains. 'It's an amazing sight. Is that Neptune's cave?' She pointed to the right-hand side of the beach.

'Yep, it sure is.'

'It looks really tiny from where we are.'

Marcie laughed. 'I suppose it does.'

'I can't believe how far I've swum!' Hannah felt proud of her achievement. Still, she knew her journey was far from over.

'You've done amazingly well,' said Marcie. 'I have to admit, I wasn't sure you were going to make it here – but you're swimming has greatly improved… for a human anyway.'

'Thanks.' Hannah disappeared to slouch down on the crystal floor with her back leaning against the balustrade.

Marcie sat beside her. 'Hey, what's up?'

'My stomach feels funny, and my head's gone dizzy.'

Marcie sighed. 'I see. Just stop worrying; it's not good for you. My mum says humans are always worrying about stuff and most of the time things turn out just fine.'

'That's easy for you to say; the sea is your home – your habitat.'

'What is it?' Marcie lowered her head to meet Hannah's, trying to make eye contact. 'Are you worried about swimming back to the cave?'

'Yeah,' admitted Hannah, staring at the floor. 'It's not going to be sea-monster-proof all the way, is it?'

'Suppose not. The best thing to do is to take one small step, or stroke in this case, at a time. Don't think about the whole picture. Just take one step at a time, and you'll be just fine. I'm sure you will.'

Hannah wiped her wet nose on her arm. 'I hope so.'

Just then, she spotted a small circular table with a mirror on it, slightly ahead of where they were sat. 'Is that…'

'My magnifying glass, yep.'

'Can I take a look?'

'Sure.'

Chapter Twelve

Hannah picked up the special-looking magnifying glass. It was an oval shape with a pink tortoiseshell back and handle. 'It's beautiful!' she exclaimed, running her fingers over the pink seashells that decorated the outside.

'Thanks. It's not just a magnifying glass though.'

'Oh!'

'Here, let me show you.'

'OK.' Hannah eagerly sat beside her, shuffling up close to see its magic.

'So, what would you like to see?' Marcie

held out the magnifying glass.

'To see?'

'Uh-huh. Like, I don't know… Would you love to see your auntie? See what she is doing right now?'

'Ooh, yeah!'

Marcie laughed. 'OK. So…' She blew her breath on the glass, then drew a love heart in the mist. 'Hey, Magnifying Glass! Please show us where Hannah's auntie is right now.'

Hannah held her breath. She hoped Auntie Meg was OK, that she wasn't worrying about her and Leo. What would she be doing? Where would she be?

As the glass de-misted, her auntie came closer and closer into view.

'Oh, no!' Hannah jumped to her feet. 'Auntie Meg's on the phone! I bet she's been searching for me and Leo and is now talking to the police!'

'Uh-oh,' said Marcie, flipping up onto her tail. 'I'm sure everything will be OK.'

'No, it won't! It won't be OK at all! What if she's told my mum and dad and they've had to cancel their business trip?' Hannah walked back and forth in a panic, wondering what to do. 'We've got to get back to the cave,' she said, despite her stomach spinning round and round. 'I need to solve the code for everyone's sake.'

'OK, let's go,' said Marcie, tucking her shiny magnifying glass into her thick plait.

Hannah waited for her to lead the way. She didn't want to be the first one landing in the endless sea of blue. 'I can't leave it any longer; Auntie Meg will be worried out of her mind.'

Marcie sprung herself onto the slide with a flip of her tail. 'See you in a –'

'W-wait!' blurted Hannah.

'Wait – what for?'

'What happens if I sink right down to the bottom of the sea, and I can't swim back up?'

'Oh, Hannah!' Marcie sighed. 'Don't think like that – you're not helping yourself. Your swimming has greatly improved, and you're much better than you think you are. You just need to believe in yourself, that's all.'

'But what if –'

'Look, whatever it is, I will come and help you. I want you to solve this code as much as you do.'

'Yeah… course.'

'Right, I'm going. I'll wait for you at the bottom.' Marcie whizzed down her slide, splashing into the sea with a fearless 'Woo-hoo!'

Before Hannah could blink or think, Marcie had already resurfaced, and it was now her turn.

'Yoo-hoo!' sang Marcie, waving her arms in the air.

Hannah gave her a quick wave, then sat down on the shiny, crystal slide and took a deep breath that pained her chest. It was the tallest, steepest slide Hannah had ever seen. It reminded her of a roller-coaster ride. The ones that gently tootle uphill in a leisurely way – and then, whoosh! Before you know it your stomachs in a whirl, your heart's leapt out of your chest and you're zooming down faster than a train.

'OK, here goes,' she said, nervously. 'Three. Two. One. W-H-O-A…!' She rocketed down the slide before landing with a big splash, deeper and deeper into the sea.

With all her might, she pushed herself forward and kicked her legs madly to reach the surface, all the while saying to herself, *I can't breathe. I can't breathe.*

Finally, she broke the surface, gasping and spluttering as the sea air reached her lungs. She'd

done it! She'd actually done it without drowning.

'Well done!' cheered Marcie, performing another backflip. 'I knew you could do it.'

'I've got a good teacher,' said Hannah, still catching her breath.

'You sure have.' Marcie grinned. 'Come on then, follow me!'

'Don't swim too fast,' said Hannah, already chasing her tail.

'Te-he! I'm sure you'll keep up.' Marcie bobbed her body and tail fin up and down, creating rippling waves behind her.

Hannah scanned the ocean, straining her eyes to see Neptune's Cave, but it wasn't visible now they were in the never-ending sea. She pelted forward to swim alongside Marcie, but the sea-girl seemed to deliberately swim faster. When she did eventually catch up, she said, 'I hope Leo's OK.'

Marcie didn't respond. She was too busy

singing again.

So, Hannah stayed silent, concentrating on her swimming stroke, and keeping her head above the salty sea water that surrounded them for miles and miles. Every now and then she'd swallow some water, causing her to cough and splutter.

'You, OK,' said Marcie, interrupting her own singing.

'Yeah,' replied Hannah, even though she was feeling out of breath and wondering how long she could continue.

Finally, she spotted a sliver of beach that she had seen from the castle, slowly growing bigger. But her arms and legs grew more and more tired, and thoughts of sea monsters sneaked into her head.

It wasn't long before the thickest of clouds returned, merging into one and colouring the blue sky black. Then the waves grew mightier, curling and rolling into a fierce battle with one another.

As Hannah fought to keep her head above the stormy sea, she spotted a ginormous black shadow in the distance, hiding beneath the surface. 'Where's it going?'

'Where's what going?' asked Marcie.

'Th-that thing!' Hannah quickly pointed. 'It's heading in our direction!'

Marcie looked over her shoulder. 'Uh-oh! You'll be a lot faster if you swim underwater like a mermaid.'

'Um… OK.'

'So, stretch your arms out in front of you with your hands together. Got it?'

'Yeah, yeah!'

'And then, with your legs and feet together, toes pointed, kick your feet in unison and propel yourself forward, bobbing your body up and down rhythmically in a full-body wave motion.'

'Oh, no!' Out of the corner of her eye,

Hannah could see the giant black thing getting closer and closer. 'We need to get out of here – NOW!' she yelled, kicking her arms and legs like a wound-up bath toy.

'Come on!' Marcie dragged her underwater before she could even prepare herself.

Hannah wriggled free, thrashing her way to the surface. 'What're you doing?' she spluttered, as Marcie sprang out from a wave. 'Are you trying to drown me?'

'Erm, no! If you want to live, you need to get going!'

'I wasn't ready.' But then Hannah spotted the gruesome monster almost upon them. 'OK, I'm ready!'

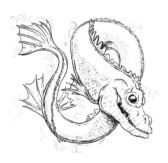

Chapter Thirteen

Quickly, Hannah dived beneath the sea, following Marcie's swimming stroke. Trying, anyway. Arms together. Legs and feet together. Bob up and down. Arms together. Legs and – Oh, it wasn't any quicker at all; it was hard work – and now she'd got a school of fish swimming in front of her. Hundreds of them – blocking her view of Marcie's tail ahead.

Unable to hold her breath any longer, she had no choice but to swim to the surface, coughing and spluttering as huge waves smashed against her tired, aching body. Then she heard an eerie sound coming from behind. Bravely, she turned her head to see a monster's swirling red eyes skimming the surface of the sea and glaring straight at her.

Her heart banged against her chest as she desperately scanned the vast ocean, wondering which way to go. She tried swimming away in the opposite direction, but the waves threw her closer and closer to the monster.

Marcie appeared, slightly ahead of her. 'Swim towards my sea pearl!' She pointed towards her pearl that had just come into view. It was the closest thing to them, but not close enough.

Hannah checked the monster's whereabouts. The huge creature had raised its enormous black head above the water, its huge nostrils sniffing the air.

She focused on swimming to the sea pearl with Marcie as the cruel waves tossed her back, showering her hair and face. Then the water went black, showing an image of the monster behind her.

As she glanced round, it seemed delighted in scaring her, showing off its hideous teeth with an evil grin. How would she make it in time? She could barely ride the waves, let alone swim to the pearl. 'It… It's g-gonna eat me!'

'Swim beneath the water with me!' Marcie gave her a nudge to get going.

So, Hannah dived beneath the sea, occasionally swimming to the surface to catch her breath as she kicked her legs like mad, propelling her faster than ever before.

Until she felt something rough and leathery against her foot. She flinched and shot up to the surface to see the monster's huge head looming down upon her.

Oh no – how would she make it to the sea pearl now? Hannah couldn't think – she struggled to breathe, and her head was in a spin.

With no time to spare, she dived beneath the

sea again, straining her stinging eyes to look for the pearl ahead.

And then with relief, she spotted it – shining bright as it lightened up the water surrounding it. Finding some energy in her tired legs, she motored herself forward even faster, hauling her aching body out of the water and climbing to the very top.

But the monster was still there, glaring straight at her as it raised its unbelievably long neck further and further out of the water to reach her.

'NO!' she shrieked, tucking her legs into her trembling body and wrapping her arms around them.

Just then, Marcie leapt above a wave. 'It's OK, Hannah. It won't come any closer because of the brightness from the pearl.'

'Oh… OK,' said Hannah, still trembling.

Marcie turned to face the monster, challenging its menacing eyes with her own fierce look 'Hey, you! Stop it!' she yelled. 'You keep away from us! Do you hear?'

With a fearsome ROAR! the monster tried grabbing hold of her fluke with its scissor-sharp teeth, but Marcie outsmarted it, whacking its huge head back into the sea. Until it reappeared again, making a deafening moan and a groan noise before dragging her into the sea for a full-on war.

Hannah gripped the shiny pearl with her feet, wondering how she could help. She couldn't leave Marcie to fight the sea monster alone. She had to do something. Before she could change her mind, she took a courageous breath and eased herself back into the titanic waves, ignoring her heart pounding as she focused on finding Marcie. But she couldn't see her anywhere. She feared the worst.

Hannah pelted back up to the surface, frantically searching for Marcie. For a split second, she saw her, until she was yanked into the depths of the sea again by the vicious sea creature.

'Right!' fumed Hannah. 'That's enough!' Bravely, she dived beneath the sea once more to help.

Poor Marcie. Her tail was being shaken around like a rag doll. How dare the big bully attack her like that; it just wasn't right. Hannah waved her arms in front of the monster's fearsome eyes, trying to catch its attention, but she couldn't. It was too preoccupied with Marcie. *C'mon, Hannah.* She panicked, wondering how she could help. *Think! Think! Think!*

Just then, Marcie began spinning in circles, around and around, faster and faster – but still, the monster didn't let go.

As Hannah watched in horror, struggling to hold her breath, she spotted the magnifying glass falling out of Marcie's hair. Remembering what Marcie had said about the monsters not liking bright

lights, she quickly swam past the beast to catch it –
and then shone the super-bright light into the
monster's troublesome eyes, causing them to shut.

The monster flickered its eyes open again,
rotating its head around and around. Still, she
continued, stretching her arm towards it, and shining
the magnifying glass even closer into its evil eyes.
After making loud groaning noises that rumbled
through the sea, the monster swam away, retreating
into the depths of the ocean.

Unable to hold her breath any longer,
Hannah shot out of the water, gasping for some air
to reach her lungs.

'You, OK?' asked Marcie, joining her.

Hannah passed her the magnifying glass.
'Yeah!' she panted, treading the gentler waves with
zero energy left in her body.

'Thanks so much for your help,' said Marcie
kindly. 'You did great.'

'I'm just glad I could help in some way. It's all my fault anyhow.'

'I guess it is.' Marcie grinned. 'But you outsmarted the horrendous sea monster, and that was pretty cool!'

Hannah grinned back. 'Yeah, I guess it was.' There was nothing to stop her now. She and Leo would soon be back home at Auntie Meg's.

That is, if she could figure out how they could get back to the cave. Her body ached so much; she could barely move a muscle. And Marcie didn't look as though she'd be able to make it either; she was now floating on her back, resting her body and torn tail.

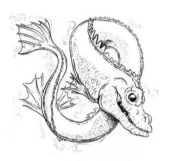

Chapter Fourteen

'I don't know about you, but I am so tired. My arms and legs are stiffening up so much, they feel like lead,' said Hannah, floating on her back beside Marcie as she allowed the calmer waves to carry her.

'I'm feeling quite tired too, and my tail feels really sore.'

Hannah glanced at Marcie's tail and flinched. 'Ooh! It's still bleeding. How are we ever going to make it back to Neptune's cave now?'

'Domitius!' called Marcie, her screechy voice travelling across the sea.

'Domit…' Hannah tried shouting, but her throat was too dry, and she started coughing.

So, the girls continued floating on their backs, hoping for Domitius or Neptune to rescue them, but there was no sign of them anywhere. There was no sign of anyone.

'If we swim slowly, we'll soon…' Hannah paused when she spotted something from the corner of her eye. 'Hey, it's Neptune!' she said, suddenly finding some energy in her aching muscles to tread water.

'Where?' Marcie flipped herself forward. 'Yay, Neptune's here!'

His almighty figure was steering something in their direction, but it wasn't a boat. As he got much closer, Hannah realised he was riding a horse-drawn golden chariot.

'Wow!' Wondering if it was for real, she rubbed her eyes and reopened them. The

magnificent sea horses were still there: four snow-white horses with golden manes and fish tails from behind. *Splish-splash-splish-splash!* went their two front legs and webbed feet as their flashing blue eyes led the way, hurtling straight towards them. 'Aww!' she gasped. 'They're so beautiful... magical.'

'Yep, they are quite something, aren't they?' agreed Marcie. 'They are Neptune's hippocamps.'

Neptune drew back on the golden reins, and the mighty hippocamps slowed to a halt before them. 'Quick!' he said, impatiently. 'Climb on!' Holding out his giant hand, Neptune helped both girls climb onto the back seat of his chariot.

'Thanks,' said Hannah, looking all around at the fairy-tale chariot. She ran her fingers over the soft, velvety cushion of her seat, feeling relieved to see a handle to grab onto. On the sides of the chariot were golden guards with the words *Neptune's*

Kingdom engraved in bronze swirly writing.

Neptune pointed his trident at Marcie's torn tail and pressed a white gem, which released an array of dazzling, tiny white stars that gleamed brightly.

'Thank you.' Marcie seemed pleased to have her cuts healed and began flipping her tail from side to side with not much thought about Hannah sitting beside her.

'There's not much time left.' Neptune looked over his shoulder at Hannah. 'You need to solve the code before we are overrun with sea monsters.'

She sighed. 'I know. I'm trying my best.'

'OK – back to the cave!' boomed Neptune, pulling the hippocamps' reins. Obediently, they bolted up onto their webbed feet and charged forward.

'Whoa!' Hannah gripped the seat handle after the chariot flung her backwards.

'You, OK?' Marcie asked.

'Yeah,' she replied, just as a rolling wave showered her hair and face.

The hippocamps hurtled through the water, their golden manes blowing in the breeze. Hannah glanced over her shoulder to see a trail of bubbly waves behind them. So, this must be what it was like on a water ride at a theme park, only much faster.

'Hey, look who it is!' said Marcie, cheerily.

With an 'Ee-Ee-Ee-Ee' Domitius leapt out of the water to the left of Hannah.

'Oh, Domitius!' she said in surprise. 'I wondered where you were!'

Domitius seemed to be smiling right back at her as he leapt over and under the gentler waves beside the chariot, then shot out of the sea, his nose pointing towards the sky.

Hannah stretched her arm out towards him,

and he jumped up even higher to kiss her hand; it was so sweet.

'Woo-hoo!' the girls chorused with a clap, which only encouraged him further as he swam around in circles, dived deep, somersaulted high and, unbelievably, walked on his fluke on the surface of the water!

Hannah let out a squeal of laughter. 'Wow! That is like… so cool!'

Marcie laughed. 'I know, he's amazing!'

'He sure is!' said Hannah, scooping her wet hair away from her face.

Domitius made a high-pitched chirping noise as though he understood and, after one final clap from the girls, he ended the show with a slap of his flippers on the surface of the sea.

The sun was now centre stage, shining down upon Neptune's Kingdom as the hippocamps continued charging through the water on a quest. A quest to take Hannah back to the cave to solve the code. She knew that. But all she could think about was poor Leo, stuck in the cave. She hoped he was OK… all by himself.

As she scanned the journey ahead, there was Neptune's deserted beach in the distance, and his cave on the right. *Oh, it couldn't be much longer now…* she hoped. *Surely.*

But then something terrible happened. One of the hippocamps seemed to get scared by something.

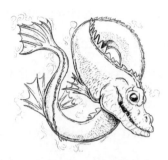

Chapter Fifteen

The startled hippocamp threw its head back and made a loud snort as though it was in pain.

The girls looked on in horror.

'Oh, no!' cried Hannah, steadying herself on the rocky chariot. 'What's happening?'

'Stay away from my hippocamps!' thundered Neptune like a storm cloud. Using his trident, he parted the sea as though there were an invisible wall between them.

Hannah covered her face with her hands, but then she couldn't resist peeking between her fingers. And there it was. A petrifying sea monster yanking the poor hippocamp's leg further into the sea and then attacking its webbed foot.

As the chariot rocked madly from side to side, Domitius sneaked down deep beneath the sea and attacked the beast with his snout, ramming its snake-like body so hard that it let go of the hippocamp's foot and slithered, half-dazed, in the opposite direction with a gruesome wail.

'Phew!' said Hannah with relief. 'The sea monsters are everywhere.'

Marcie nodded in agreement, looking worried.

'Good boy!' Neptune patted Domitius on the head before aiming the trident at the hippocamp's torn webbed foot. Once again, tiny silver stars shot out of the three prongs like stars on a sparkler – circling its foot and miraculously healing yet another wound. 'Now, we've no time to spare!' he said, pulling gently on the reins. 'Back to the cave!'

Trouble was… The hippocamps didn't seem to want to gallop anymore. Instead, they gently paddled through the sea with their webbed feet in unison, glancing this way and that as though they were scared of being attacked again. This made the voyage far more relaxing, like being on a paddleboat, yet endless at the same time, and Hannah was now desperate to get back to the cave to see Leo. Hopefully, he'd just fallen asleep on Neptune's chair.

Neptune must have thought they'd been travelling for long enough too because he pulled on the hippocamps' reigns again to encourage them to speed up – and they did. They galloped once more through the sea.

'Whoa!' said Hannah, grabbing hold of the handrail again. As she fixed her eyes on the journey ahead, Neptune's cave was almost upon them. To the left of her was the beautiful beach with sand as white as sugar, twinkling like millions and trillions of tiny stars.

Finally, they arrived back at the cave, and the hippocamps slowed down to paddle under the archway, stopping beside the cave's rock bed with a neigh!

Neptune's towering body rose as he held out his huge hand and helped Hannah step onto the rock bed.

'Thank you,' she said, racing towards Leo, who was now curled on top of a gold pebble beside the rock pool. 'Oh, Leo, you're still here!' Holding him out at arm's length, then drawing him in close, she kissed the top of his fluffy head. 'Oh, I'm so pleased to see you! Have you missed me?'

'Meow!' Leo's huge eyes looked up at her as though she'd deserted him.

'Oh, I'm sorry.' After stroking his fluffy body, she placed him back down on his favourite

pebble just as Marcie joined her with several flips in the air towards the rock pool.

'I see your tails fully healed then,' said Hannah, smiling at her.

'No time to chat,' interrupted the God of Sea. 'The monsters are multiplying! You need to solve the code before my kingdom is destroyed!'

'I know, I know,' she murmured, despite wanting to yell and scream at him for making stupid codes up in the first place. Didn't he know that she wanted to solve it more than anyone… so she could return home to Auntie Meg's with Leo.

'I've got to go now,' stated Neptune. 'I'll leave you with the trident.' Placing the trident on the rock bed, he sat back down on his chariot and grasped the hippocamps' reins.

'But –'

'Come on – quick now!' said Neptune to his hippocamps, totally ignoring Hannah.

Hannah stared in disbelief as they whooshed out of the cave, Neptune already disappearing into the vast ocean. 'They come and go so quickly,' she said, sighing heavily.

'Yep, they take care of all the innocent sea creatures, you know.' Marcie passed the magnifying glass to Hannah. 'But they won't be able to keep the monsters at bay forever.'

'Yeah, yeah – I get what you're saying,' said Hannah, feeling as if the world was against her.

'Hey, I'm sorry. I'm not trying to upset you.'

Hannah managed half a smile, then stared down at the inscribed gold pebble, her eyes glossing over. What would happen if she couldn't solve the code? Would she and Leo be stuck at Neptune's Kingdom forever? She couldn't bear the thought.

As she placed the magnifying glass over the inscribed gold pebble surrounding the rock pool, Marcie leaned over it too, eager to see.

'Good luck,' said Marcie, obstructing Hannah's view.

Hannah tried nudging her out of the way to see, but then a small clownfish jumped onto the end of Marcie's tail, and Leo stepped onto another pebble to paw it. The trouble was, she didn't want him falling into any more rock pools, like *ever!*

'C'mon, you.' She picked him up and gently placed him at the other side of her, away from the rock pool. Only the cheeky kitty took no notice and pitter-pattered towards it again. After a deep sigh, she decided it was no use; she would just have to let him be whilst figuring out how to solve the code.

Suddenly, Leo gave a high-pitched 'meow!' before hiding beneath Neptune's chair.

'Hey, what's up?' asked Hannah, concerned.

'Meow!' was all he could say, his hair bristled like a brush.

'Uh-oh!' said Marcie, climbing out of the

rock pool. 'Something's broken into the rock pool!'

Chapter Sixteen

'What!' shrieked Hannah, her shaky hands covering her mouth as a monstrous black head rose out of the rock pool, disturbing all the pebbles surrounding it.

Everything but her heart froze as the monster looked all around; its serpent-like neck twisting and turning until it caught sight of Hannah and stopped. It completely stopped. Glaring at her with a wicked grin as if it knew she was scared.

'Wh-what now?' She turned towards Marcie for help, but even she looked scared.

'I... I don't know!' was all Marcie could say, curled up in a small space.

Hannah's feet wouldn't budge as literally the biggest sea monster *ever* gripped the side of the rock pool to climb out, causing some pebbles to fall in.

'Oh, no – the pebble!' She'd never know which was the special pebble now. The ones that hadn't fallen into the rock pool were all piled up in a heap – and what if? What if it hadn't escaped falling in and was already sinking to the bottom of the sea?

She'd got to find the pebble before it was too late. But she struggled to move. It was as if her body belonged to someone else. Even worse, it was becoming more impossible to get past the monster. Still, she had to do something – and fast!

Taking a deep breath, she bravely hurried past, chucked the magnifying glass on Neptune's chair, and grabbed hold of the mighty trident, preparing for war.

Leo stared up at her from beneath the chair, his eyes wide with fear.

'It's OK, Leo,' said Hannah, desperately hoping so. 'S-stay there.' But when she turned around, the creature had fully escaped the rock pool and was fiercely thrashing its tail from side to side nearly whacking her in the face.

There was nowhere for her to go except to take a step back beside Leo, panting as the cold, damp rugged cave wall dug into her back and cold seawater seeped through the cracks in the ground, trickling over her toes.

'EEEEEOWWWFFTZ!' Leo pounced onto the monster's tail and dug his sharp claws into its thick flesh.

But still the monster continued and was now swinging poor Leo from side to side viciously. It seemed Leo had no choice but to release his claws and jump down onto the flooded rug.

Hannah's fear turned to anger towards the despicable monster. How dare it treat little kitty like that? So, keeping hold of the trident, she dodged past the monster's swinging tail to sneak up on its left, water now swishing around her ankles. Luckily, it appeared not to notice as it snooped every space and crack, looking for something – anything to scare.

Then the beast of all monsters sniffed and lowered its head towards Marcie, rolled up in a ball. And with a deafening, 'Growl!' that sounded like thunder, it showed off its prehistoric teeth.

Any minute now and it would be tearing into Marcie's tail for lunch, and Hannah wasn't gonna let that happen, so she bravely waded through the water. 'STOP!' she yelled. 'Don't you dare scare my friend!'

Slowly, the monster turned its gruesome head in Hannah's direction, causing stalactites to break from the cave ceiling with an almighty splash to the ground. Then the monster stretched its snake-like neck even more and came so close to her that she felt it must surely be able to hear her heart pounding and smell her fear.

Despite a prickly, tingling sensation spreading through her hands and fingers, she kept hold of the trident with all her might, hoping it would deliver. But she wasn't sure which button to press, and before she'd even had a chance to fire, the monster had licked its ghastly teeth and swooped her and the trident up into its cave-sized mouth with its big fat tongue.

'Aaaaaaargh!' Hannah clung onto the trident as she slid further and further down the monster's foul-smelling tongue, her stomach heaving. It stunk! And now her ears were throbbing from the loud groaning noises coming from the monster.

Still, she was determined more than ever to win the war. Finding some strength, she used the trident like a bar, placing it on the raised lumps and bumps of its slimy green tongue, then pulled herself up as if it were a climbing wall at the park. Slowly, she hiked her way up, but it wasn't easy. The monster's tongue was moving all over the place and she had to grab onto whatever she could.

When Hannah finally reached the opening of its enormous mouth, she spotted Marcie between the gaps of its triangular teeth, gliding through the rising water to save Leo before placing him onto Neptune's chair and retrieving the magnifying glass.

Hannah rolled the trident off the monster's slithering tongue and watched it fall with a splash into the water. Now it was her turn. Her heart quickened at the mighty height, but she had to do it – before it was too late.

So, as Marcie shone the magnifying glass at the monster's eyes, it gave a loud bellowing, 'ROAR!' and Hannah jumped.

'Whoa!' She fell awkwardly into the water

before quickly hitting the hard ground with a thud. 'Oww!' she cried, jolting her back. But she couldn't just sit there in the cold water, almost covering her mouth. The magnifying glass wasn't getting rid of this beast; it seemed defiant and angrier than ever. So, tilting her head back out of the water, she scrambled around on her hands and feet, desperately searching for the trident.

Marcie ducked her head under the water and then shot up. 'It's here!'

'Great,' said Hannah, quickly stretching her arms out for the trident. 'I'll take it from here!' She wasn't allowing her to take over this time.

'Oh… OK,' said Marcie, seeming surprised as she reluctantly passed it her.

'Thanks,' said Hannah, pointing it towards the gruesome thing. 'Which –?'

'Try the burgundy gem!' replied Marcie as she continued blinding the monster's eyes with the magnifying glass.

Aiming the trident like a gun, Hannah pressed the button and purple powder blasted out from the three tines, causing the monster to give an ear-splitting moan and a groan as it shrank and shrank, until eventually turning into purple dust floating in the water, just like a coloured bath bomb.

Marcie smiled at Hannah, clearly enjoying the victory, and Hannah returned a smile as all the water disappeared through the cracks and whooshed back into the sea.

Still, it was far from over.

Chapter Seventeen

Hannah searched desperately for the special gold pebble, hoping it was still there and hadn't fallen in as she rummaged through a heap of pebbles beside the rock pool.

Marcie checked through another pile. 'I can't find it here,' she said, her tail wrapped around her body as she sat beside her.

Hannah's fear of not finding the pebble grew as she let out a heavy sigh. 'It's not in this lot either,' she fretted. 'It must have fallen into the pool, but I can't see it.'

Marcie plunged her head into the water for

what seemed like ages, then shot back out.

'Any luck?' said Hannah in anticipation.

'Nope,' said Marcie, stroking her hair as though it was a comforting teddy. 'It's possible it could have moved with the tide and settled on the ocean floor.'

'Oh no – I hope not!'

'Yep, me too,' said Marcie. 'Hopefully, we can find it before it drifts too far.'

'I… erm… I'm not sure I'll be able to swim down to the bottom,' began Hannah. 'I'll get out of breath and –'

Marcie leapt up onto her tail and grabbed some kind of mask off the cave wall. 'Here, this will help!' She threw it towards her.

'What's this?' Hannah inspected the mask that looked more like a space helmet. 'It looks very hi-tech.'

'It is! It's a Neptune Ninja Mask. It covers

your entire face, allowing you to breathe underwater for hours,' explained Marcie, as though she'd rehearsed it.

'Um. Great... I think,' said Hannah, although she wasn't really sure of the idea. The last thing she wanted to do was spend hours under the sea. Still, she placed the mask over her face to show Marcie.

Marcie grinned. 'It suits you!'

'Hmm,' groaned Hannah, quickly pulling it off. 'I'd rather wear a sunhat.'

Leo joined in with a 'Meow!' – tilting his head at her as though he wondered what was happening.

'Will he be alright?'

'He'll be fine,' said Marcie. 'Neptune said as much.'

'I hope so.' Leo seemed fine; he was now preoccupied with clawing at Neptune's chair and making pull marks in the fabric, but still... she couldn't help but worry about him. 'You stay there, my little kitty. It's safer for you.' She kissed the top of his delicate head, hoping she'd be OK too. If she couldn't save herself, she couldn't save Leo. 'Right, let's go,' she bravely said, her whole-body trembling at the thought of another unknown adventure. 'You are coming with me, right?'

'Sure,' replied Marcie, giving her plait one final stroke. 'I know the bottom of the ocean like the scales on my tail. I'll help you find the pebble.'

'Thanks,' said Hannah before placing the ninja mask over her face. She could see clearly through it and even breathe normally, but she couldn't turn her head so easily. Still, it was all she'd got. And in order to solve the secret code, she'd got to find the inscribed gold pebble – before it was too late. Ignoring her heart pounding and the blood rushing through her veins like a super-fast car on a racing track, she gave Marcie the thumbs up.

Marcie winked in acknowledgement, then gracefully dived into the rock pool, her fluke already disappearing from sight.

Hannah quickly followed, swinging her legs around into the pool before taking the plunge to dive down deep. As she pelted her way further and further into the sea, she felt relieved to see Marcie's bright blue tail, rhythmically swishing up and down, up and down.

But Hannah didn't want to stay behind her all the way. No. So she practised her mermaid stroke, swimming faster and faster – bobbing the lower half of her body up and down just as Marcie had shown her.

Only then she lost sight of Marcie as oodles of coloured fish swam towards her in the opposite direction. They were literally everywhere. Thousands of them. Swimming over her. Swimming under her. In between her legs and touching her toes. Some looked as though they'd been splashed with paint, others were covered in stripes like the patterns on a zebra. Many of them swam in schools, as though on a mission, and others kept changing direction. Maybe they were lost? Just like Hannah. She couldn't help but panic more and more as they continued to surround her. Oh – where was Marcie? Would she even know that Hannah wasn't behind her anymore?

After eventually escaping the last school of fish, she searched like mad for Marcie – to the left and to the right, straining her eyes to focus as far as she could see. Then finally, she saw her tail swishing from side to side.

Hannah felt a huge sigh of relief as she kicked her legs even faster through the water, determined to catch her up. When she did, Marcie smiled and waved at her, probably unaware that she'd just lost her to a flurry of fish.

As they swam deeper and deeper, the pale blue sea became darker and Hannah's body much colder. How long would she survive before her bones stiffened up? Still, she had to keep going. If she just kept moving her arms and legs, she'd be OK.

Then, in the distance, she spotted patches of brightly coloured coral reefs where different-sized fish were swimming through. As Hannah got closer, she realised they had reached the seabed; it was covered in sand which meant they couldn't have strayed too far from the seashore. But where was the inscribed gold pebble? Surely, it was close by.

As the girls searched all around, Hannah spotted something drifting behind some purple coral. She gave Marcie a gentle nudge and pointed in the direction of where it had landed. Eagerly, the girls swam over the coral reef to investigate.

Hannah wiped the sand away to reveal a

shiny inscribed gold pebble. It had to be the special pebble – it just had to be! As she held it up for Marcie to see, she nodded in agreement, so Hannah scooped it up and clasped it in her hands for safekeeping.

Chapter Eighteen

Hannah hadn't a clue which way they should be heading back to the cave. Although they were close to the seashore, it was quite disorienting because every direction she looked in, there were patches of coral with small fish swimming through.

Marcie must have noticed Hannah looking lost because she beckoned her forward to follow her. Then she stretched her arms out above her head, pointing them towards sea level as her tail rhythmically swished back and forth, back and forth on their journey to the top.

It wasn't so easy for Hannah to swim though

as she had to keep a tight hold of the gold pebble which was quite heavy. Still, she managed it somehow, madly kicking her legs against the power of the water.

Oh – how much further is it? worried Hannah. It seemed to be taking forever to reach the surface.

But then the dark blue sea became lighter and warmer… and then warmer still. Feeling a surge of energy to keep going, she propelled herself forwards, faster and faster, until she finally broke free from the ocean. Flinging off her mask, she gasped for the sea air to reach her lungs.

'Here, let me take that for you,' said Marcie, holding out her hand for the mask. 'You're not going to be able to swim well carrying them both.'

Hannah passed her the mask. 'Thanks,' she said, still catching her breath. It seemed Marcie did have a kind side after all.

She'd still got the pebble to carry in both hands though, which meant her legs had to do all the work and they were beginning to stiffen up. Ignoring the pain, she focused on the strip of pure white beach in the distance, slowly growing bigger. It looked like the perfect paradise island – and she couldn't wait for her feet to touch the sandy bottom.

As they got much closer, she started doggy paddling, stretching her legs out in every direction.

Marcie turned round at her. 'What are you doing?'

'I'm trying to feel the bottom.'

Marcie laughed. 'We're not quite there yet,' she said, sounding like a swimming teacher. 'Come on, keep going. Only five more minutes.'

Although it wasn't five more minutes at all. It might have been for Marcie if she were swimming on her own, but for Hannah, it seemed more like an hour before they finally reached the shallow water.

When they did, Hannah allowed the wet sand to support her wobbly legs and tired feet. 'Oh – I'm so pleased we've made it to the seashore,' she said, gazing at the beautiful beach as gentle waves swished around her knees.

'Did you ever doubt me,' said Marcie, grinning.

'Um. Kind of,' teased Hannah. 'No – of course not. I just doubted myself.'

Marcie laughed. 'Seriously though, don't doubt yourself,' she said. 'You're capable of a lot more than you think.'

'Yeah… I guess so,' said Hannah, smiling. She was beginning to realise that.

Lowering her hand into the clear blue water, she splashed it onto her legs, just like she did when she was five. Maybe the sea was a beautiful place… in some ways. Then she strolled out of the sea carrying the inscribed gold pebble before flopping down on the beach.

Marcie joined her, swishing her tail from side to side in the bubbly water.

'Hey – look who it is!' exclaimed Hannah, spotting a tiny ball of white fluff merging with the colour of the sand as he scampered towards them from Neptune's Cave. 'It's Leo!'

'Meow!' With a purr, he climbed up onto her wet sandy knees.

'So, my little kitty,' she said, ruffling the tufty fur on top of his head. 'What have you been up to?'

Leo just tilted his head to one side, his big saucer eyes staring innocently up at her.

'Oh – I'm sorry for leaving you in the cave again all by yourself,' she said, gently stroking his fluffy fur.

Leo responded with another meow as if to say it was OK and then licked her hands with his

rough tongue.

'Ah, it looks like he's forgiven you,' said Marcie, smiling.

'Yeah…' Which made Hannah think… 'I hope Auntie Meg forgives me.'

'Forgives you for what?'

'Oh, I don't know.' Hannah sighed. 'She's probably wondering where I've been all this time, especially if she's taken a trip down to Morvoren Beach, seen my flip-flops there and me and Leo are nowhere to be seen. I bet that's why she rang my mum and dad and they're probably worried out of their minds too and –'

'Hey, slow down,' said Marcie, raising her hands in the air. 'You don't even know if she's rang your mum and dad.'

'No, it might have been the police instead!' said Hannah, panicking. 'I don't know which one's worse… I guess neither really.'

'Everything will be OK, I'm sure,' reassured Marcie.

'It will if I can figure out this inscription.' Hannah placed Leo on the sand beside her and tried reading the curly writing on the pebble but then remembered. 'Did you bring –'

'Oh no, the magnifying glass!' said Marcie, placing her hands over her eyes. 'I'm sorry, I forgot. I left it beside the rock pool when we were looking for the pebble.'

'It's OK,' said Hannah, rising to her feet with the ninja mask and gold pebble in hand. 'C'mon, Leo, we need to get back to the cave – so I can read this inscription and hopefully solve the code.' She turned to Marcie, hoping she'd be joining her, but she'd disappeared.

'Oh, yoo-hoo!' Marcie shouted, waving from the crest of a wave. 'I'll race you there!'

'All right – you're on!' Hannah called back.

Leo didn't need telling twice. He was already making tiny pawprints in the sand as he ran towards Neptune's Cave.

'Don't be too late,' jested Hannah, grinning.

'Te-he!' Marcie laughed. 'That's fighting talk!'

Hannah laughed back. 'It sure is!' she said before sprinting through the soft, powdery sand. If she didn't win the race, she could at least give her mermaid friend a challenge. And with one final leap through the arched entrance of the cave, she saw that Marcie had already arrived.

'You beat me!' said Hannah, panting as she rested her hands on her knees.

'Te-he.' Marcie giggled. 'I didn't come first though.' She nodded her head at Leo curled up on Neptune's rug, grooming himself. Then she somersaulted towards the rock pool to retrieve the magnifying glass.

Hannah placed the pebble and mask on the soggy wet rug before picking Leo's purring body up. 'Oh – who's a clever boy then,' she said, kissing his cute little nose and then placing him back down beside her.

With Marcie and Leo for company, Hannah knelt in front of the inscribed gold pebble, hoping this time she could solve the code.

'You can do it!' encouraged Marcie, handing her the magnifying glass.

Just then, Neptune rode into the cave on his chariot, his beautiful white hippocamps obediently stopping with a 'Neigh!' at the water's edge.

'Now then, Hannah,' he boomed, his giant figure striding onto the cave floor before sitting down on his chair with the trident. 'You have proven to be a good swimmer, shown courage, and determination and worked well as a team,' he began, his eyes fixed on hers. 'But I can't send you home until you've solved the code.'

'I know,' was all she could say. Despite wanting to scream and shout at him that this wasn't fair... To be held captive just because of one pebble being dislodged from his rock pool. But what good would it do? And where would it get her? She'd just be stuck in his kingdom forever.

Chapter Nineteen

Hannah placed the magnifying glass over the tiny writing and then cleared her croaky throat to read,

'Thoughts have power – they're energy.
By solving this code, you will see,
thoughts become things,
so make yours loving,
and you shall have wings.'

'Hmm... I've no idea what it means,' she said with her hands clasped behind her head. 'The words

look like gobbledygook to me.' She glanced at Neptune, hoping he'd shed some light.

'I'm sorry,' he said, shrugging his huge shoulders. 'I can't help you.'

'Maybe the words are just jumbled up or something,' suggested Marcie.

'Um… maybe,' said Hannah, but the more she stared at the inscription, the more puzzled she was.

'You're thinking about it too much!' said Neptune.

Hannah sighed. 'Yeah, I know… It's hard not to.' It didn't help that she could feel his eyes boring into hers.

'You just need to clear your mind for a moment,' he went on.

'OK.' So, she did. She closed her eyes and took deep breaths in and out to help clear her mind. *Re… lax,* she said to herself, over and over. Then she thought about the times she and Becky had made up secret codes together, just for fun. Their codes were simply their notes to each other spelt backwards. With that in mind, she opened her eyes again and began to read the inscription, back to front.

'Thoughts have power – they're energy.
By solving this code, you will see,
thoughts become things,
so make yours loving,
and you shall have wings.'

'That sounds lovely,' she said. 'But what does it mean?'

'It isn't important what I think. It's about what it means to you,' replied Neptune. 'So. Tell me. What have you learnt?'

Hannah thought about how far she'd come…

overcoming her fears and even learning how to swim like a mermaid. If only her mum and Auntie Meg had seen her swimming in the sea – they'd be so proud. Which made Hannah feel proud too and her heart filled with a newfound confidence in what she could achieve if she just took the first step and believed. Believed in herself.

'I've learnt that if I face my fears head-on, they become much smaller and less scary, until eventually they can lose their power over you altogether, just like the sea monsters,' she proudly said.

Neptune nodded in approval. 'Go on,' he encouraged, gesturing for more.

'Also, if you fill your mind with loving, positive thoughts you will attract loving, positive situations back to you – leaving no room for fear.'

Neptune allowed a smile to break free underneath his messy moustache as he rose to his huge feet and boomed, 'That's it – that's exactly it!' while clapping his almighty hands together. 'Well done – you've solved the code and have clearly learnt a lot!'

Her heart overflowed with joy that spread throughout her whole body. She felt so much relief to know that she would finally be going home…

Until Neptune added, 'But you can't go home until you've returned the pebble.'

'What?' said Hannah in disbelief. 'But I have returned the pebble. It's right here.' She pointed to the obvious.

'You must place the inscribed gold pebble back where it belongs, among the pebbles surrounding my rock pool. This will then form a magic circle once again, protecting my undersea kingdom with love and happiness.'

'But I can't put the pebble back until I go home; the rock pool is on Morvoren Beach.'

'The rock pool on Morvoren Beach is the same as the one on Neptune's Bay; it's a portal rock pool, giving you access to both places,' he explained.

'Ah…! OK. That's cool… I think.' Hannah turned to Marcie. She felt a blend of excitement and sadness at the same time; excited to be returning home to Auntie Meg's, yet sad to be saying farewell to Marcie. She would miss her terribly. As Hannah looked into her friend's watery eyes, it was clear that she felt the same. In fact, she had never seen her look so sad before, not even when they were fighting the sea monsters. 'Thank you… For everything. I couldn't have solved the code without you.'

'No. Thank *you*.' Marcie sniffled before flinging her arms around Hannah and squeezing her tight. 'You've saved our kingdom.' As her eyes brimmed with sorrow, a tear trickled down her face and splashed onto the rug. Then the tear shone and gleamed brightly before transforming into a shiny pearl.

'Whoa!' Hannah gasped. 'That's amazing!' She'd never seen anything like it before.

'Here,' said Marcie, holding it on the palm of her hand. 'Take it; it's a magical mermaid pearl.'

'Thank you!' Hannah ran her fingers over the glossy pink pearl. 'Thank you so much – it's beautiful!'

'I'm glad you like it,' said Marcie, smiling as she wiped her eyes dry. 'It's a reminder of our friendship, so keep it safe.'

'I will!' Hannah reassured her. 'I'll put it into my costume pocket for safekeeping.'

Marcie smiled and her freckled cheeks puffed up. 'Hopefully, see you again?'

'Um. I'm not sure.' Hannah glanced at Neptune, but he stayed silent. 'You know, before I met you, I would have said no way! But we've swum so much and done so much and now… I don't feel scared of the sea anymore. If there are no more sea monsters to fight, then I'd love to come back and visit you.'

'Ah, that would be brill!' said Marcie, her eyes twinkling. 'I'd really like that!'

The girls shared a smile and wrapped their arms around each other until Neptune interrupted with a loud cough – making it clear that it was time for Hannah and Leo to go home.

'Now, as I was saying… You must stand in the middle of the rock pool on Neptune's Bay and place my inscribed gold pebble back where it belongs, which is in a special place surrounding the rock pool. You will know when the pebble is correctly placed because stars will appear. When they do, hold your mermaid pearl, and say, "Take me to Morvoren Beach." You will then be transported back.'

'And that's it?' said Hannah in surprise.

'That's it,' he confirmed with a nod.

She glanced back at her mermaid friend, eager to share her joy.

'That's great, I'm so pleased for you,' said Marcie, smiling back with her thumb in the air.

'OK,' said Hannah. 'I'm sure I can do that.'

'Good,' he said. 'You can go whenever you're ready.'

'Did you hear that, Leo?' She turned to the adventurous little kitty, but he'd disappeared to the rock pool and was now playing catch with Cardea the Crab as she crawled back and forth from the pebbles.

Marcie grinned at Leo. 'I think Cardea likes him.'

Hannah laughed. 'Yes, I think so too, but no more dramas today, Leo. I think we've had enough adventure for the entire summer,' she said, gently nudging him towards the cave entrance with the pebble in her hand. 'It's time for us to go home.'

With a big yawn and a lazy stretch, Leo pitter-pattered alongside Hannah towards the entrance, where Neptune was already waiting.

'Hope you get back OK,' called Marcie, now sitting beside the water's edge to dip her tail in.

'Thanks,' said Hannah, waving goodbye to her.

Chapter Twenty

Hannah looked up at Neptune, standing before her. 'Thank you for helping me overcome my fears,' she said, smiling. 'You've taught me a lot.'

'Indeed,' boomed Neptune, his huge body leaning forward to shake her hand. 'And remember, it's OK to be scared of things, but running away from them can make them more frightening than they actually are.'

'Yeah, you're so right,' agreed Hannah. 'I can see that now.'

'And, Leo,' began Neptune, kneeling to shake his tiny paw. 'Thank you for guarding my cave – you did a grand job!'

Leo's innocent face stared up at him with a cute 'meow!' and the god of sea smiled in a way that Hannah hadn't seen up until now. Maybe he wasn't so bad after all.

'Well…' began Neptune, clearing his throat as though he wasn't quite sure what to say anymore. 'Good luck, Hannah!' he eventually said before pointing towards the beach outside his cave.

'Thanks,' she said, feeling so much better about herself than when she arrived; like there was nothing she couldn't do if she just put her mind to it.

As she and Leo strolled out of the cave together, the soft sand caressed her feet, and the pleasant heat from the sun soaked into her skin like a warm comforting blanket. Before entering Neptune's Kingdom, she'd forgotten how good it felt to be walking on the sand without being afraid of the seashore. While sauntering along, she buried her toes in the sand and flicked it into the air – just for fun.

Then, she heard a magnificent SPLASH! 'Hey, Marcie!' she cheered, her heart filled with joy for her new mermaid friend.

'Bye.' Marcie gave her a wave as she dived in and out of the playful sea.

Hannah waved back before sprinting after the cheeky kitty who had decided to run off again. 'Leo, wait!'

Luckily, he stopped when he reached a rock pool that looked quite familiar.

'Oh, clever boy!' she said, staring at the special-looking rock pool. 'So, this must be Neptune's rock pool; it's got gold pebbles surrounding it.' Gazing into the rock pool, a fear of the unknown stirred in her stomach… Would she really end up back at Morvoren Beach? Or somewhere else? But then she remembered what

Marcie had said… Just take one step at a time and you'll be fine.

So, she did. She took a big girl breath and stepped into the middle of the rock pool with Leo, looking all around the edge for where there was a gap the same size as the pebble, just like a missing jigsaw piece.

'It's there!' she rejoiced, jumping in the air as if she'd just won a prize. Carefully, she placed the pebble back in its rightful place, her hands shaking slightly from the uncertainty of what would happen next. She quickly picked up Leo, making sure he wouldn't stray again. Then magical, tiny silver stars appeared, twinkling brightly like the stars in the sky as they danced around and around above the gold pebbles.

'Wow,' she whispered in awe, her whole-body tingling. It felt like being in the middle of the starry sky.

Leo's fur bristled like a brush. 'Meow!' he said, pawing at the pocket on Hannah's swimming costume.

'What? What's up?' Then she realised. 'Oh no – the pearl!'

'Meow!'

'Where's it gone?' Panicking, she felt inside her pocket. Outside her pocket. Everywhere, until she realised there was a hole in her pocket.

'Oh, no!' Hannah's heart shrank like a popped balloon and a tear ran down her cheek. 'It's gone.'

Soon after the stars stopped twinkling too, their bright light fading until they disappeared altogether.

'Oh, I'm so sorry, Leo.' She sniffled, wiping her wet nose with her hand. 'What are we going to do?' Wrapping her arms around Leo tight, she stared down at the water in the rock pool, her head pounding with worry. How would they ever get back home now?

Just as she was beginning to lose all hope, the water began swirling and whirling around her feet, faster and faster as it spun around. And then in the distance, she spotted someone out of the corner of her eye. It was Neptune standing at the cave entrance, aiming his trident directly at them. As he did, tiny silver stars shot out of the trident and twinkled towards them, showering them from head to toe.

Soon, she felt lightheaded… and drowsy… And then she must have blanked out or something because she couldn't remember anything after that, until finding herself in the middle of the rock pool on Morvoren Beach, still half-dazed and feeling dizzy. She held her tender head and then rubbed her eyes as though she'd been in a deep sleep…

But where was Leo?

Hannah breathed a sigh of relief when she saw him. He was creating tiny footprints in the sand as he pitter-pattered towards Auntie Meg's cottage. Slowly, she stepped onto the sparkly sand to join him. *Hmm… How strange*, she thought, looking all around. The beach was still deserted, and her flip-flops were in the same place. *Oh well…* She shrugged. Maybe no one visited the beach today.

'Oh, come here, you,' she said, picking up Leo and wrapping her arms around him. 'You're staying with me for the rest of today.'

With a purr and a swish of his tail, Leo buried his fluffy head into her arms as they headed towards the steep steps of Auntie Meg's cottage.

Hannah glanced over her shoulder to see the rock pool, but it had gone. She scanned the entire beach as far as her eyes could see, but it wasn't there. How weird – it had disappeared!

'Well, at least you can't go exploring the

rock pool anymore!' she said, smiling at Leo's cute kitten face. But he couldn't see or hear her; he'd fallen asleep. Probably dreaming about another adventure.

As Hannah climbed the steep steps towards the cottage, she wondered what her auntie might say. After all, they had been gone for some time. In any case, she wouldn't be telling her about Neptune's Kingdom. No way.

When Hannah reached the top, she turned round to admire the scenic view of the beach and beyond. *Cornwall and... Neptune's Kingdom really was a beautiful place!* She smiled at the thought before hurrying towards the cottage.

With Leo still soundly asleep in her arms, she tried opening the door quietly, but his ears pricked up, and he leapt out of her arms towards his milk dish.

'Hello!' Hannah called out sheepishly to her

auntie, half expecting her to be in a state of panic, wondering where she and Leo had been.

'Oh, Hi, love,' called Auntie Meg from the living room. 'I'm just on the phone to your mum.'

'Oh...' said Hannah, disappointedly. She knew it! She just knew she'd ring her mum. It was hours ago now that she spotted her on the phone through the magnifying glass. They must have been on the phone for ages. 'What, still?' she couldn't help but say.

Auntie Meg raised her eyebrows in surprise. 'I've only been on the phone for five minutes!' she said with a chuckle. 'Ay dear, I don't know. I think your daughter would like a word,' she said to Mum before passing the phone to Hannah. 'You have a word with your mum now and I'll speak to her after, OK?'

'Um, yeah, OK. Hi, Mum...' As she chatted to her mum, she breathed a sigh of relief. It became apparent that she hadn't a clue where Hannah had been. So, she told her all about the fun time she'd had on the beach with Leo. But of course, she didn't mention Neptune's Undersea Kingdom – or the fact that she could swim like a mermaid in the deep blue sea.

'Thanks, Auntie Meg. I've finished.' Hannah passed the phone back, then dashed upstairs to her bedroom. As she gazed out of her bedroom window, she watched the carefree waves roll onto the sparkling, honeycomb sand. 'Oh, I'm sorry, Marcie,' she murmured, feeling the hole in her pocket. Hannah couldn't believe she'd lost her magical mermaid pearl.

At that moment, something fluttered towards her bedroom window and stuck to the outside. As Hannah quickly retrieved it, she saw it was a golden envelope addressed to her. Excitedly, she jumped onto her bed and ran her tingly fingertips over the words, *Neptune's Undersea Kingdom* that were embossed all around the edge, then carefully opened the shiny, golden letter…

Greetings, Hannah,

Thank you for helping to save Neptune's Undersea Kingdom. By solving the code, you have helped defeat the sea monsters and brought back love and happiness into my sea world.

And remember, it's OK to be scared of things, but running away from them can make them seem more frightening than they actually are. Always try to face your fears if you can.

Then perhaps. . . just like magic, they will transform from being a scary monster into nothing more than a speck of dust, eventually disappearing out of sight altogether.

So, take care and keep your thoughts positive – by doing what you love.

Regards,

Neptune

P.S. Please find enclosed your mermaid pearl; Marcie says you dropped it on Neptune's Bay. Keep it safe, as it has magical powers.

'Oh wow – no way!' Hannah's mouth fell open in disbelief as she stared at the gold letter and the magical mermaid pearl that had just fallen out. 'So, Neptune's Undersea Kingdom really does exist!' With a big smile, she kissed her mermaid pearl in the palm of her hands, then placed it back in the envelope with her letter.

'Oh, Hannah!' called Auntie Meg from the bottom of the stairs.

'Yeah,' she said, quickly placing the envelope inside the secret pocket of her suitcase.

'How come Leo's wet?'

'Erm, he kind of…' Hannah skipped downstairs to join her auntie. 'Ran onto the beach and had a paddle in the sea.'

'A paddle – he's soaked through!'

'Yeah, I know... Sorry about that…' Hannah paused, not quite sure what to say. 'I rescued him though,' she said, grinning proudly.

'Oh, well done!' cheered Auntie Meg. 'You look wet too. Did you dive in?'

'Erm… yeah, kind of.'

They both shared a laugh.

'Auntie Meg.'

'Yes, love?'

'Please could you fix the hole in my pocket?' She showed Auntie Meg the hole in the pocket of her swimming costume.

'Of course I can. What happened?'

'Oh, it's a long story,' she replied, winking at Leo.

Some more books by Genna Rowbotham

Ellie-May & her Toy Dragon, Ben

Rhyming Picture Book
Ages: 3 – 5

Lottie, the Ladybird's Adventure

Fantasy Chapter Book
Ages: 7 - 9

Where is Lamby?

Rhyming Picture Book
Ages: 3 - 5

You can find out more at **www.gennarowbotham.co.uk**

Genna Rowbotham started her career as a secretary and has since founded GR Typing Services, an online secretarial business. Inspired by her children, in 2017, she wrote her first story and is now the author of ten books as well as a short story published in the magazine, *Brilliant Brainz.* Genna has a passion for writing stories that entertain, educate and inspire young ones so they can escape the seriousness of life and enter a world of magic.

She lives with her husband and lively, imaginative daughters in Derbyshire in a house full of books, magazines and all sorts of artwork from her children (empty cereal boxes are often taken from the recycle bin to reinvent something wonderful like a spy camera or a telescope).

When Genna's not writing, she loves reading, star gazing, movie nights, and exploring the great outdoors with her family.

You can find out more about Genna's books on her website at www.gennarowbotham.co.uk

Thanks for reading. If you enjoyed this book, please consider leaving an honest review on your favourite store.